Addie Malone, brave [...] of Shotgun Ridge in [...] see the town's bustling [...] nearly extinct. But thanks to the efforts of four smug, matchmaking old men, Shotgun Ridge was bursting at the family seams once more. Now it was time for a new bachelor roundup—and proud, fierce sheriff Cheyenne Bodine seemed just the man to lead the stampede to the altar!

* * *

"That's my bed. And I'm dying to know why you're in it."

Emily frowned. "I think there's been some kind of a mistake. Unless we've both leased this house, there's obviously a question over who has dibs on this bed."

Cheyenne's grin was slow and incendiary. "I assure you the house—and that bed—belong to me. Although giving you 'dibs' on it has a certain appeal."

His voice was incredibly soft, incredibly thrilling. Cheyenne Bodine was a sexual man. But she wasn't here for sex. And as huge and uncomfortable as she was, it should have been the last thing on her mind.

Should have been.

Dear Reader,

Welcome to Harlequin American Romance, where you're guaranteed upbeat and lively love stories set in the backyards, big cities and wide-open spaces of America.

Kick-starting the month is an AMERICAN BABY selection by Mollie Molay. The hero of *The Baby in the Back Seat* is one handsome single daddy who knows how to melt a woman's guarded heart! Next, bestselling author Mindy Neff is back with more stories in her immensely popular BACHELORS OF SHOTGUN RIDGE series. In *Cheyenne's Lady*, a sheriff returns home to find in his bed a pregnant woman desperate for his help. Honor demands that he offer her his name, but will he ever give his bride his heart?

In *Millionaire's Christmas Miracle*, the latest book in Mary Anne Wilson's JUST FOR KIDS miniseries, an abandoned baby brings together a sophisticated older man who's lost his faith in love and a younger woman who challenges him to take a second chance on romance and family. Finally, don't miss Michele Dunaway's *Taming the Tabloid Heiress*, in which an alluring journalist finesses an interview with an elusive millionaire who rarely does publicity. Exactly how *did* the reporter get her story?

Enjoy all four books—and don't forget to come back again in December when Judy Christenberry's *Triplet Secret Babies* launches Harlequin American Romance's continuity MAITLAND MATERNITY: TRIPLETS, QUADS & QUINTS, and Mindy Neff brings you another BACHELORS OF SHOTGUN RIDGE installment.

Wishing you happy reading,

Melissa Jeglinski
Associate Senior Editor
Harlequin American Romance

CHEYENNE'S LADY
Mindy Neff

HARLEQUIN®

TORONTO • NEW YORK • LONDON
AMSTERDAM • PARIS • SYDNEY • HAMBURG
STOCKHOLM • ATHENS • TOKYO • MILAN • MADRID
PRAGUE • WARSAW • BUDAPEST • AUCKLAND

To Carol Miller,

For birthday lunches and adventures, hours of talking and
solving all the world's problems (we ought to have it
straightened out by now, don't you think?) and for a
cherished friendship I treasure deep in my heart.
I love you, girlfriend.

ISBN 0-373-16898-5

CHEYENNE'S LADY

This edition published by arrangement with Harlequin Books S.A.

® and TM are trademarks of the publisher. Trademarks indicated with
® are registered in the United States Patent and Trademark Office, the
Canadian Trade Marks Office and in other countries.

Visit us at www.eHarlequin.com

Printed in U.S.A.

ABOUT THE AUTHOR

Mindy Neff published her first book with Harlequin American Romance in 1995. Since then, she has appeared regularly on the Waldenbooks bestseller list and won numerous awards, including the National Readers' Choice Award and the *Romantic Times Magazine* Career Achievement Award.

Originally from Louisiana, Mindy settled in Southern California, where she married a really romantic guy and raised five great kids. Family, friends, writing and reading are her passions. When not writing, Mindy's ideal getaway is a good book, hot sunshine and a chair at the river's edge at her second home in Parker, Arizona.

Mindy loves to hear from readers and can be reached at P.O. Box 2704-262, Huntington Beach, CA 92647, or through her Web site at www.mindyneff.com, or e-mail at mindyneff@aol.com.

Books by Mindy Neff

HARLEQUIN AMERICAN ROMANCE

644—A FAMILY MAN
663—ADAM'S KISS
679—THE BAD BOY NEXT DOOR
711—THEY'RE THE ONE!
739—A BACHELOR FOR THE BRIDE
759—THE COWBOY IS A DADDY
769—SUDDENLY A DADDY
795—THE VIRGIN & HER BODYGUARD*
800—THE PLAYBOY & THE MOMMY*

809—A PREGNANCY AND A PROPOSAL
830—THE RANCHER'S MAIL-ORDER
      BRIDE†
834—THE PLAYBOY'S OWN MISS PRIM†
838—THE HORSEMAN'S CONVENIENT
      WIFE†
857—THE SECRETARY GETS HER MAN
898—CHEYENNE'S LADY†

*Tall, Dark & Irresistible
†Bachelors of Shotgun Ridge

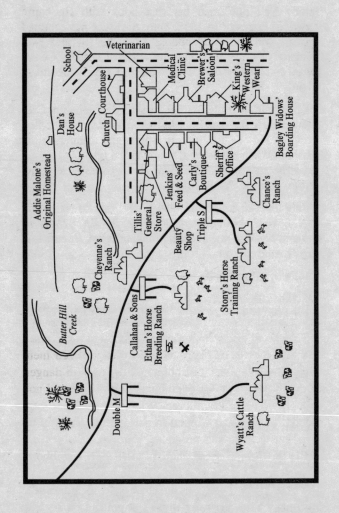

Prologue

"Well, Vanessa, me and the boys are making a pretty good go of this here matchmaking business." Ozzie Peyton gazed at the portrait of his late wife, which held a place of honor over the stone fireplace. He still discussed every little thing with his sweet Vanessa—though he didn't like to spread that around. Some folks just didn't understand.

The "boys" were Lloyd, Henry and Vern, the four of them affectionately known as the geezers. Ozzie didn't mind the term; in fact, he kind of liked it.

They were on an important mission, had taken matters into their own hands when they'd realized their small Montana town of Shotgun Ridge was in danger of dying out due to an overabundance of men and not enough women and children. Why, the good Lord intended for men and women to pair off in twos, fall in love, get married and procreate, you bet.

But the durn bachelors here in town were a stubborn lot—clearly in need of a nudge here and there.

"Now don't go to fussin'" he said to Vanessa's portrait. "You know my mind's slippin' a bit of late and these old hands aren't quite what they used to be. Why, a mixup in address numbers is an honest-enough mistake.'' He gazed into Vanessa's timeless eyes, the eyes of a schoolteacher who could reprimand with a single look. He placed a hand over his heart, duly repentant.

"Okay, okay, it was pure-dee deliberate. But Cheyenne Bodine was always close to your heart, darlin'. Why, if it weren't for you, that boy would never have turned out so fine. And Emily Vincent—you remember her, don't you, love? A little scrapper, that one, and a bit of a jinx if you recall, but wait till you hear what she's gone and done now.'' Ozzie rubbed his hands together, couldn't contain the smile that spread across his face. It was a smile Vanessa loved—she always told him his eyes twinkled.

"It's all in the family, you see. And if ever there was the perfect lady for Cheyenne Bodine, it's Emily Vincent. So we—me and the boys—figured it'd be best for everyone concerned if we got them under the same roof. Neither one of those kids knows a lick about babies—yet.'' He winked at Vanessa and was certain her lovely lips curved in response.

Chapter One

Sheriff Cheyenne Bodine got a bad feeling when he came home to his modest five-acre mustang ranch to find a snazzy Mercedes parked in the driveway, its front tires resting in the grass as though the brakes had been a little faulty. Or else the driver was under the influence of a controlled substance.

A three-quarter moon lit the cold October sky, illuminating his four-bedroom house. The fact that this all belonged to him chased away the loneliness he'd been feeling lately. Well, *some* of it.

Still, loneliness aside, he hadn't expected company. In the small town of Shotgun Ridge, Montana, Cheyenne knew the make, model and owner of just about every vehicle, and this one wasn't familiar.

The pretentious car with Washington plates stuck out like a prissy lady in a bawdy bordello.

Suspicious by nature—compliments of his job—he slid out of the four-wheel-drive Bronco, his dog hopping to the ground beside him. The smell of fall air, hay and horses wrapped around him like a familiar blanket, yet something appeared amiss in his neat world.

He cautiously pushed open the front door of his house. A blast of warmth from the furnace made his cold cheeks burn.

"Heel, Blue," he said quietly to the Siberian husky who was never far from his side.

Brows drawn together in a frown, he followed the trail of luggage and female articles through the front hall to his bedroom.

Great, he thought, picking up a snakeskin boot and a white parka that smelled ultrafeminine, some wise guy had gotten him a stripper. He sniffed again. The innocent scent of vanilla emanating from the downy fabric didn't jibe with that image.

When he reached the open bedroom door, his booted feet froze and his mouth dropped open.

A woman was sound asleep in his bed.

And this high-class Goldilocks was pregnant as all get-out.

He moved closer to the bed, his cold fingers clenching around the soft leather boot he still held.

Emily Vincent.

His heart thudded as memories flashed. She'd lived in Shotgun Ridge for a while, but her family had moved during her senior year in high school. Her departure had left a hole in Cheyenne's life.

Although he'd mostly watched her from afar, she'd been full of spit and vinegar, and he'd been half in love with her. She'd had a penchant for being in the wrong place at the wrong time and had more than once been the center of scandal, her reputation suffering, even though he'd suspected she'd been innocent.

It was the darnedest thing, as though trouble came knocking at her door.

And once again Emily Vincent appeared to be in the wrong place.

In his bed.

And if she knew the thoughts he was thinking about her as she slept—scratch that, if the *townsfolk* knew what he was thinking, her reputation would once again be the subject of discussion.

Blue bumped his cold nose against Cheyenne's hand. He gave the dog a pat to let him know there wasn't any immediate physical danger.

Now, mental danger was a whole different matter….

Easing into a chair beside the bed, not bothering to remove the sheepskin jacket that covered the sheriff's star pinned to the front of his uniform shirt, Cheyenne settled in to give his fantasies an all-expense-paid spree.

A DETERMINED LITTLE FOOT lodged under her ribs and Emily groaned, stretching out to get more comfortable. The last weeks of pregnancy were worse than she'd anticipated.

She moaned softly and opened her eyes.

The sight of the man and dog sitting beside her bed sent adrenaline straight to her head, making her dizzy, forcing a scream that came out more like a squeak.

Scrambling for the covers, she snatched them to her chin.

"No need for modesty. Aside from the boots, the rest of your clothes are still on you, though the skirt's hiked up a bit."

"Cheyenne?" She jerked at the hem of her wool maternity skirt. It had only ridden up to midthigh, thank goodness.

"One and the same, trouble."

Trouble. He'd been the only one to call her that and make it sound like an endearment rather than a judgment.

Emily released her death grip on the blankets, and placed a protective hand over her stomach. *Everything will be okay, now.*

"So," he drawled, his tone exceedingly pleasant, "mind telling me what you're doing in my bed?"

Still groggy, heart pumping, it was a moment before Emily's confused brain kicked in.

And when it did, relief was washed away by the flood of all-too-familiar emotions. The fear. The sorrow. The reason she was here. The sheer terror of what lay ahead.

But why was Cheyenne Bodine telling her she was in *his* bed?

And oh, Lord, time had been *very* nice to this sexy man. The last time she'd seen him, she'd been seventeen and he'd been twenty.

That had been fifteen years ago.

Dark hair brushed the collar of his sheepskin jacket, and deep-brown eyes focused on her with an intensity that made her want to fidget. He was a tall man, with the strong bone structure of his Cheyenne ancestors.

Silent and watchful, he emanated danger and oozed sex appeal.

Her palms were damp and her insides trembled.

She struggled to sit up, uncomfortable with their respective positions—she in the bed, him watching her like a polite panther, full of self-confidence and patience.

He immediately reached out to help her, the perfect gentleman even though his gaze was still a bit wary.

"Thanks. I feel like one of those children's toys, you know? The ones that wobble but don't fall down? Problem is, I wobble and roll and have a devil of a time getting vertical."

His piercing gaze slipped to her hugely rounded tummy, then to the naked ring finger of her left hand. Though his lips didn't curve, amusement shimmered briefly in his eyes. "When are you due?"

"In about three weeks."

"And you've come home for a visit?"

His tone clearly stated he was still waiting for an explanation. Well, he wasn't the only one. Shotgun Ridge was a friendly little town, but for heaven's sake, the man was standing in her bedroom!

"Yes, I'm here for a visit, sort of. But what are you doing here?"

"I live here. That's my bed. And I'm dying to know why you're in it."

She frowned. Was he teasing her? "Look, I think there's been some kind of mistake. Unless we've both leased this house, there's obviously a question over who, exactly, has dibs on this bed.''

"Leased it, huh? From whom?"

"Ozzie Peyton."

His grin was slow and incendiary. "I might have known those old geezers were involved. I don't know what they were thinking, but I assure you the house—and that bed—belong to me. Although giving you 'dibs' on it has a certain appeal.''

"Oh, for heaven's sake, I'm as big as a moose!"

"I have a good imagination."

His voice was incredibly soft, incredibly thrilling. Dear Lord, he was quick. And apparently very serious.

She didn't want to expand on this conversation. Truthfully, she was horribly out of practice with the flirting routine.

Cheyenne Bodine was a sexual man, always had been. But she wasn't here for sex. And as huge and uncomfortable as she was, that should have been the last thing on her mind.

Should have been.

Just went to show the potency of one Cheyenne Bodine!

Flustered, nervous, she reached for her leather attaché case and rooted around for the lease agreement she'd been sent by the mayor. "I have the paper right here. And I checked the house numbers before I came in."

He took the form from her and lazily scanned it as though he had all the time in the world and nothing at all was amiss.

"Easy-enough mistake. The numbers are off by one digit. This address is for the place next door."

"Oh, Lord, I'm sorry. It was dark—I thought I checked the numbers. I'm so embarrassed." She tightened her hand around the leather satchel, holding it in front of her like a shield—which wasn't easy, given the size of her stomach.

"I haven't unpacked yet. It'll just take me a minute to clear out and move next door." She was rambling, talking fast, but she couldn't help it. His watchful silence was making her a nervous wreck.

And just as when she'd been young, she'd made another mistake. What was it about this town? She'd been jinxed the entire time she'd lived here, star-crossed and accident-prone until the day she'd moved away.

"Now there's where you're going to run into a bit of a problem."

"Why? I asked Ozzie Peyton for something close to you. Do you object to me being your neighbor?"

"I probably wouldn't if it were a possibility. The place next door burned down several years back. The house was on my property, I used to rent it out, but after the fire, I couldn't see any sense in rebuilding."

No wonder Ozzie Peyton had told her the house she'd thought she'd leased was furnished. Of course it was—with Cheyenne's furniture.

She was starting to feel thoroughly ungrounded. She'd been so tired when she'd come in that she'd just fallen into the bed, never looking around to see what was what. Now she did peruse her surroundings.

Masculine, definitely, decorated with touches of his Native American heritage. She saw a photograph on the dresser of a man and woman, the woman's hair as dark as a raven's wing, the man's as bright as the sun. And standing beside the couple were two little boys— one with the dark, striking features of his mother, the other as fair as the father.

Cheyenne and Jimmy Bodine.

Brothers who'd been estranged from each other over pride and a stupid mistake.

Tears stung her eyes and throat.

Jimmy had displayed that same photograph in his bedroom.

"Hey, trouble." Cheyenne leaned forward and touched her cheek, his thumb gentle as he caressed the fragile skin beneath her eyes. "No need to get upset. We'll work something out."

She shook her head. "I'm sorry. It's been a trying time for me lately." She reached for his hands and held them in hers. "It's not just baby hormones making me emotional. I'm afraid I have some bad news." She squeezed his hands, said as gently as possible, "Jimmy's dead."

His fingers tightened against hers, nearly crushing her bones. His eyes flared, his head shaking in denial. "No..."

"I'm sorry."

"How? When?"

"An accident on the highway. Two weeks ago. A semi hit a patch of black ice and caused a pileup."

She saw his throat work on a swallow, his gaze slipping to her pregnant stomach.

"Why wasn't I notified?"

"I'm sorry. That was my fault. I was so stunned, in a fog." Tears slipped down her cheeks. "I'm sorry," she whispered again, the words horribly inadequate. "Jimmy was so excited about..." She couldn't go on, simply pressed her hand to her stomach.

"You're carrying Jimmy's baby?"

She nodded. Her world was in a mess. She was grieving and terrified and very mixed up. She'd run the gamut of emotions lately—some that even shamed her. A good deed, prompted out of deep, unconditional love had come to a tragic end and altered the steady course she'd chosen for herself—and oh, God, she was so selfish to even think about that now.

Cheyenne shrugged out of his coat and moved to sit on the side of the bed. "Blue, stay," he said when the dog started to follow.

The mattress dipped under his weight. He put his arms around Emily and held her, as much for his own comfort as for hers. His heart felt as though it was ripping in two.

But he'd learned at a young age to shield his emotions. If the dirt-poor half-breed had dared to show any vulnerability, he'd been fair game for ridicule and trouble.

Because of his distinctive features, he'd fared better on the reservation than Jimmy, with his buttery hair, had. But in the Anglo world, it had been different.

Always the butt of a joke or sneer. Children could be so cruel.

Perhaps that was why he'd tried so hard to fit in, to make something of himself, to show everyone he wasn't a dirty Indian whose father hadn't stuck around and whose mother had taken her own life after her husband had divorced her and taken her youngest son with him.

And because of his desperate need to fit in, to prove himself, he'd pulled away from Jimmy, his own brother, his flesh and blood. He'd been so pompous and unbending, so caught up in honor that he'd turned his back on his brother when trouble had come knocking that last time, had allowed the estrangement to continue long after the rift should have been repaired.

And now there were no second chances. That knowledge settled like a burning rock in his gut.

Jaw tight, he held Emily to his heart. She'd obviously had a part of Jimmy—a very big part of him, he realized as the baby shifted in her womb, pressing against his side. Her heartache would be as great as his. Perhaps even greater.

"He was your husband?"

She shook her head, her silky hair brushing his chin. He frowned, his gut clenching.

"He didn't honor you with marriage when you learned of the pregnancy?"

She leaned back in his arms, gazed up at him. "Oh, no. You misunderstand. Jimmy was married to my sister, Debbie."

"Ah, hell."

"Stop it, Cheyenne." She pulled back, sniffed and swiped at the tears that had slid down the curve of her jaw. "I'd think by now you'd have learned not to jump to conclusions. The wrong conclusions."

Her tone was testy, a mother hen sticking up for her chicks. In this case, the chick was his brother. But Emily Vincent had always been that way. She was a champion of the underdog. Probably because she'd been a bit of an underdog herself. An underdog who, by the look of her clothes and car, had come out on top.

"I'm pretty confused here."

Emily sighed, annoyance vanishing like a cloud whisked away by a swift moving breeze. "Of course you are. And that's my fault. The babies are a product of a surrogate agreement between the three of us— Debbie, Jimmy and me."

"Babies?"

"Twins."

"Oh, man."

The masculine terror in his tone nearly made her smile. Nearly. Because she felt that terror herself. Every time she thought about the enormous responsibility that lay ahead of her, she broke out in a cold sweat.

Especially now that she was alone.

It wasn't supposed to be this way.

"For health reasons that are still a little complicated for me to try and explain, Debbie couldn't carry a baby full-term. They wanted their own family so badly I agreed to help them out."

"That's a hell of a sacrifice. An incredible gift."

She shrugged. "It was only nine months out of my life. Or *was*."

He stroked her hair, sat with her in silence for several minutes.

"You lost your sister in the accident, too, didn't you?" he asked quietly.

She nodded, trying to battle back the overwhelming grief.

His hand stroked her back, caressed her shoulder. "God, I'm sorry, Em. How long were they married?"

"Three very happy years—aside from the sadness of several traumatic miscarriages. This was their dream, Cheyenne. They were thrilled about the babies. We all were. Every step of the way, every change in my body, the first fluttery kick, the tests—we went through it together." What she didn't mention was that the farther the pregnancy progressed, the more the babies had felt like a part of *her*—that she was more than merely an incubator.

The strength of those feelings had frightened her. She loved her sister, knew how desperately Debbie had wanted that child—these children. Emily had even dreamed of having her sister offer to let her keep one of the babies.

But in her saner moments, she knew that was ridiculous, that her hormones were simply playing tricks on her. She didn't know the first thing about parenting, didn't *want* to know. She was a career woman, for heaven's sake. Her life was full and happy and that was that.

Then, in the blink of an eye, Debbie and Jimmy were gone. And Emily had been faced with choices. A few of them—the ones she'd guiltily considered in the deepest, darkest part of the night—were too awful to even think about.

She shivered and Cheyenne rubbed her arms. "Want me to start a fire?"

"I'm okay. I'm sorry I didn't contact you about the funeral. It was all handled so fast. I didn't stop to think that you might have wanted to make different burial arrangements…because of your heritage."

"Jimmy was more white than Cheyenne. He didn't embrace the principles or covenants of our people."

"But you do."

"In my heart. Not always in practice."

"I had them buried side by side in Washington."

"That's as it should be." He stood and went to gaze out the window. So silent. So still.

She knew he was battling emotions over his brother's death. It was horrible enough for her, but she'd had a few weeks for the numbness to wear off, to try to adjust. And she counted her blessings every day that she'd had these last years with Debbie and Jimmy.

Cheyenne hadn't. That had to be tearing him up.

She moved up behind him, placed her palm gently against his rigid back. He didn't stiffen or try to evade her touch, but neither did he react.

The three-quarter moon glowed like a misshapen yellow ball, somehow both sad and eerie. An image of a lone wolf, baying its heartache, sprang to her mind.

Oh, God, she hurt for him. He was like that imaginary wolf. Alone. Isolating himself the way he'd done as a boy. Internalizing his pain and facing life with a spit-in-your-eye facade.

But she saw past the shield—there had always been an uncanny, inexplicable connection between them, even though they'd barely known each other. She felt his pain as though it were a living breathing entity in the room with them.

"Did you eat?" he asked quietly, and she nearly jumped.

"No, but—"

"I'll go fix us something."

"That's not—"

He turned then, and the agony in his obsidian eyes tore at her heart, made her throat ache. She would have put her arms around him, but he stepped away.

"I need a few minutes," he said softly, hesitating only long enough to brush her cheek in compassion and apology before he walked out of the room, the gray husky following like a silent, trusted friend.

Emily swallowed hard, her heart a stinging mass of sorrow—for herself, as well as Cheyenne. She imagined he needed more than a few minutes, but knew that was all he'd allow himself. Physically there wasn't a trace of the boy left in him, but she remembered what he'd been like all those years ago.

A proud warrior suffering in silence.

Chapter Two

The scent of vanilla wafted around him. A scent both innocent and classy. Cheyenne slid the bowl of left-over spaghetti into the microwave and punched in two minutes on the timer. He didn't have to turn around to know that Emily had come into the kitchen.

He glanced at her. Her arms were crossed over the shelf of her huge belly—Lord, it looked like it was painful—her hands rubbing the soft texture of her sweater sleeves. Cashmere. Expensive.

Yes, Emily Vincent had come a long way from the skinny little freckle-faced scrapper with a mop of frizzy hair.

The hair was still a bit wild, curling at will, but it had a sort of sophistication about it.

"Cold?" he asked. To him, it felt like the furnace was set too high, but Emily kept hugging herself as though the October winds had breached the seal of his storm windows.

She came across the room, stopped right next to him and looked up, her green eyes filled with a compassion he wanted to drown in. But he couldn't let himself.

"I'm fine," she said softly. "Are *you* okay?"

He couldn't seem to look away. He wanted to bask in this woman's presence, wanted to wrap her in his arms and let her console him, to console her in return.

He resisted. He'd learned long ago not to reach beyond his limitations, learned to keep his emotions and his yearning in place.

"I'm fine."

"Cheyenne. Don't."

Just two words and she nearly unmanned him. "Ah, hell, trouble. It hurts." He pulled her to him, rested his lips against her forehead.

"I know," she whispered.

They stood there for what could have been hours, but was only minutes. Sharing the pain made it lessen. Or else it was Emily's presence.

The babies somersaulted in her stomach and he jerked back.

She laughed and he knew his face must have appeared stunned.

"Does that hurt?" He'd been around pregnant women before—Shotgun Ridge certainly had its share of them lately—but he'd never been in a position to feel this kind of activity, up close and personal, so to speak. He'd never had the occasion to really ask about the miracle of carrying a child—children in this case— in a woman's womb.

"Sometimes it does if they get a foot or hand under my ribs. And with two of them in there, I feel a bit like an overloaded packhorse carrying a ten-pound centipede."

She took his hand in hers and placed it on her stomach. The babies were doing acrobatics. What felt like an elbow or knee protruded beneath her skin, rippling along his palm.

"May I?" he whispered, and when she nodded, he placed his other palm against her stomach, cradling her, awed, stunned, so moved he felt he needed to sit down.

These were his brother's babies.

He did sit down then, pulling her with him onto his lap.

For a minute she resisted, held herself rigid in surprise. Gradually she settled on his thighs, easing against his chest as they shared the miracle of what was taking place inside her body.

"Do you know if they're boys or girls?"

"I'm not a hundred percent sure. They were sort of hugging each other when we did the sonogram, and we couldn't get a clear look at their little body parts."

He grinned. "At least they were loving each other, instead of fighting."

"Yes. That's much easier on my insides, for sure."

"Do they sleep much?"

"No. And neither do I. I hope that doesn't foretell what they'll be like when they're out here in the world."

He raised a brow. "Did it bother your sister that you'd accepted her husband's seed?"

She glanced down at him. "You're not thinking I had sex with Jimmy, are you?"

"Well, no." Actually he didn't know what to think.

"These babies are truly Debbie and Jimmy's."

"Of course—"

"No, truly," she said. "Technology is absolutely amazing nowadays. They took Debbie's eggs and fertilized them with Jimmy's sperm in some little dish in a lab. I think. I didn't really concern myself with that end of things. I just figured they'd call me when it was my time to step up to the plate."

"It must have been a jolt to end up with twins."

"Well, yes, I'd only counted on carrying just one baby, even though I knew they'd implanted two eggs. In most of the cases, I'm told that this sort of thing doesn't take right away, and I guess they often put more than one in to increase the odds. For my sake, Debbie only agreed to just the two implants. Evidently the hormones they gave me primed my body perfectly, because both embryos took hold right off the bat and here we are."

Yes, he thought, *here we are.* She seemed to be thinking the same thing because she went quiet. He tightened his arms around her, the fuzzy material of her sweater tickling his forearms.

Glancing down at him, she gently ran her vanilla-scented palm over his cheek, a soothing touch that said she understood. And she did.

Then she scooted off his lap, using the table to aid her in standing, and tugged her sweater lower on her hips, rubbing her palms along her sides as though she wasn't quite sure what to do with herself or her emotions.

"Did you say something about feeding us?"

He rose, wondering why she seemed so uncomfortable all of a sudden. "Yes. Nothing fancy. Just leftover spaghetti and salad. I didn't know I'd be entertaining."

She gave a soft laugh. "I guess you were a little surprised to come home and find a woman in your bed."

"A little." Understatement. He took the bowl of pasta and sauce out of the microwave and set it on the table. "Sit and eat."

"You don't have to ask me twice. Seems like that's all I want to do lately. Eat."

"Well, you're eating for three."

"Oh, pu-leeze. I'm trying to contain my hugeness to just the middle of me. I've got a whole closet full of business suits I need to fit back into."

The mention of business clothes reminded him of the total package of this woman. The car, the air of class and money. A woman of substance.

A career woman who just happened to be pregnant with his brother's children…and her sister's.

Technically he and Emily were the uncle and aunt of the children she carried. He was having a little trouble coming to terms with that.

He poured milk into two glasses, put a salad and bread on the table, along with the pasta, and sat down.

They ate in silence, and for all her proclamations about being hungry, she ate very little.

"Something wrong with the spaghetti?"

She shook her head. "It's very good, thanks. I think it's all these emotions swirling around inside me."

He nodded. "Since you went to the trouble of leasing my house—"

"I didn't know it was yours!"

He smiled gently. "I know. I was teasing."

"Oh."

"But your actions indicate there's more on the agenda than just delivering the news about Jimmy. So why are you here, Emily?"

She took her plate to the sink, ran water over the porcelain, then put the dish on the counter and turned.

"I need help, and I didn't know where else to turn. I'm a marketing director for an advertising agency. I'm not equipped for motherhood, and I'm in over my head here." She paced, bracing a hand on her back as though it ached. "How in the world am I supposed to cope with two infants? One would have been difficult enough."

"You could give them up for adoption," he said softly.

She halted, glanced at him and then quickly away. "I could never do that. I love these children. They're part of me. And part of my family."

He nodded. "And mine."

"Yes," she said softly, "and yours. That's why I came to you. I need you to help me out with the babies—at least until I get the hang of things."

"You want money."

"Darn it, aren't you listening to me?" Her voice rose in exasperation. "I'm an executive. I drive a Mercedes Benz. I have plenty of money, but no family or know-how. The thought of what lies ahead terrifies me right down to my toes. I don't know squat about babies. They weren't supposed to be mine. I was only the oven to cook them in!''

Cheyenne noted her manicured nails, highlighted blond hair and quality clothes, as well as the panic in her voice. ''Why didn't you just stay put and hire a live-in nanny? You look and sound as if you can afford it. Why come all the way out here and ask for my help?''

She pushed her hair behind her ears and sighed. ''Because of Jimmy,'' she said softly.

He felt the word like a punch in the solar plexus.

''Can we, um, go sit somewhere?'' she asked

He noticed that she was rubbing her back again and he swore. The poor woman looked like a strong wind might blow her over. She'd hauled in suitcases, had probably been driving for hours and had only gotten a short nap before he'd woken her.

He led her into the living room and settled her on the couch while he built a fire in the river-rock fireplace that spanned one entire wall. When the flames were licking and spitting, he adjusted the screen and sat in the overstuffed wing-back chair across from her. Blue settled himself in front of the hearth, head resting on his paws, eyes alert as though gauging the uncertain atmosphere in the room.

''I met Jimmy several years ago when he applied for a job at the advertising firm I work for,'' she began. ''I didn't recognize him at first, but then I put the name together with the face.''

Cheyenne nodded. ''Jimmy was staying with our

father in Wyoming most of the time you lived here in Shotgun Ridge.''

"I know. It was only after a while that I realized he was your brother. You guys don't look a lot alike.''

A raven and a dove. Just like him and Emily. Cheyenne was darkness. Emily was light and bright and effervescent.

"Jimmy and I easily became friends, and then I introduced him to Debbie. It was like something out of a storybook with them. They were so much in love. For the longest time Jimmy didn't talk about his family…about you.''

She looked uncomfortable admitting that and he eased her with a nod. "We were both pretty hard-headed.'' He rubbed a hand over his face. "God, I regret that.''

"So did Jimmy,'' she said softly.

His heart actually jolted. "What are you saying?''

"After the babies were conceived—'' she smoothed a hand over her stomach "—he told me about your estrangement, about the money he stole.''

Cheyenne glanced away, stared at the flames. "He came to me and confessed.'' Confessed that he'd stolen from the elderly affluent couple he'd been doing handyman chores for. "He wanted me to hide him until the speculation died down.''

At the time Jimmy had only been seventeen, and Cheyenne, at twenty-five, had felt so much older, so damned superior. The timing couldn't have been worse. He'd just applied for a deputy position in Shotgun Ridge. He'd been so determined to rise above his impoverished beginnings, so determined to do right. He'd been disgusted by Jimmy's actions, ashamed, afraid of how his brother's crime might affect his own goals.

"I wanted him to turn himself in," he said. "We fought about it."

"I know. He stole because he was hungry."

Cheyenne's head jerked. "For drugs, you mean?"

"No. Food."

Surely…

"He was proud, too, Cheyenne."

Cheyenne closed his eyes. Damn it. "Our father was providing for him."

"No. Your father was drinking. The rent was due. Jimmy was scared."

He felt as though drops of acid were pelting his heart. "And I was so pompous and rigid I didn't take the time to listen." Was it because he'd felt abandoned by the father Jimmy lived with? Blond and blue-eyed, Jimmy looked like their father. Cheyenne looked like the son of an Indian.

And Chuck Bodine had come to hate that, denying that he, too, shared a trace of the same Native American heritage. He'd wanted his boys to be replicas of him, obviously figured he had a fighting chance since the woman he'd married was actually one-quarter Anglo, perhaps banking on those recessive genes to give him the all-American family he envisioned.

His father had been a man with grandiose dreams without the drive to follow through.

Cheyenne wanted to believe that his parents had

been in love. But poverty, low self-esteem on his father's part and interference from his mother's family
had torn the family apart, divided the camps. Fiercely
protective, Cheyenne had aligned himself with his
mother. Jimmy had moved to Billings with their father.

Jimmy had been the one who'd suffered, pulled between the divorced couple. And Cheyenne had been
helpless to stop the downward spiral that had begun
to take place in Jimmy's life because of it.

"You didn't turn him in," she pointed out gently.

Cheyenne shrugged.

"It wasn't solely your fault. Jimmy said he let you
think the worst of him."

He leaned forward and plowed his hands through
his hair. "There was a time when we were so close.
God, forgive me."

"I'm sure He does. And so did Jimmy. He idolized
you, Cheyenne. But he, too, had way too much pride.
He was ashamed of what he'd done, but it was probably the best thing that ever happened to him. He
turned his life around, got an education. He was a
fabulous artist, and our company snapped him up in a
hurry. He did all the artwork for our ad campaigns.
And after he and Debbie got married and the pregnancy came about, he really started yearning for family. He wanted to mend fences, Cheyenne."

"Why did he wait?" *Why did I wait?*

"He wanted to wait until the babies were born, to
come to you and proudly show off his family, a visual
testament to how he'd turned his life around."

"I should have made the first move." Actually he had. Several months after he'd landed the deputy position, he'd tried to contact Jimmy, attempted to reconcile. But Jimmy had rebuffed him, wouldn't have any of it.

"'Should have' won't change anything now."

"I know." But that didn't alleviate the guilt. He should have pushed. Should have tried harder. He glanced down at her stomach. "So what now?"

She leaned forward, having to spread her thighs in order to accommodate her belly. "Now I seem to have a housing crisis."

"You're really serious about me helping you out with the babies?"

"I've taken maternity leave, packed up most of my clothes and personal stuff and driven five hundred miles. It doesn't get much more serious."

"Why me?"

"You have a stake in these children's lives."

"I could always visit."

She stood up and paced. Stopping in front of the fireplace, she said, "I'm scared."

He rose, too, moved closer. "It's more than that, I think."

She glared at him, but there was no heat behind the look. Only discomfort.

"Come on, trouble. Why did you come to me?"

"I'm a sucker," she muttered. "Besides the fact that I panicked, I—I guess I thought I could mend the rift between you and Jimmy."

"How?"

"By reuniting you through the babies. I loved Jimmy, Cheyenne. And so did my sister. They talked about this reunion, looked forward to it." She shrugged as though her incredible intentions were no big deal. "But I *do* need the help," she quickly added.

He couldn't take his eyes off her. He was so touched and awed, astounded by this woman's unconditional capacity for love.

This was her gift to his brother.

And to him.

He couldn't imagine any other woman being this selfless. And he was truly baffled that she didn't appear to see how unique she was.

But then, Emily had always been like that.

As though it had happened yesterday, he remembered a time when they were young. He'd been the teenage kid with the chip on his shoulder, the outcast. His family hadn't had enough money for lunches and he'd gone without. Emily, three years younger than him, had scooted up next to him on a bench where he'd isolated himself and casually shared her sandwich with him as though they met for lunch like that every day. She didn't speak or make a big deal. She was just this little fourteen-year-old skinny girl who'd rescued him.

Funny how that memory had stuck with him all these years.

Now she was the one who needed rescuing.

"Say something," she said nervously.

"Thank you."

She let out a breath, gave him a smile. "I still seem

to be in a dilemma over housing. I can't believe the mayor deliberately leased me a house that had burned down—and wasn't even his to begin with. No wonder he didn't ask for a deposit—unless he didn't know about the fire?''

"He knew. How much did you tell him?"

"About what?"

"Your reasons for wanting to take up residence close to me?"

"Um, pretty much everything. I told him about the babies and Jimmy and Debbie... Come to think of it, that man has a way of getting people to spill their guts."

"Crafty son of a gun."

"But what in the world was his purpose?"

"Matchmaking."

"Excuse me?"

"They're on a campaign. Half the town is."

"But I'm not looking for a man."

He raised a brow. "You came looking for me."

"Oh, for heaven's sake, you know what I mean. So put me out of suspense here. Can I stay with you? Will you help me get through the first couple of months with the babies?"

"I see a couple of problems there."

"Well, bring them on. I'm good at problem solving."

"Really? Is that what pays you enough money to buy a Mercedes?"

"The Mercedes is leased. But yes, I do put out fires, so to speak, and yes, I'm paid very well for it. When it comes to marketing, everyone's got a gripe. So lay yours on me.''

''I don't know a thing about babies.''

''And you think I do?''

''You're a woman.''

''Give the man a star for astuteness. Just because I'm female doesn't make me qualified. And there are *two* of them!''

Her tone was so horrified he nearly smiled. ''I'm sure you're a quick study.''

''Likewise. Cheyenne, what is the problem here? These children are your blood.''

''I know, damn it! I'm scared, too.''

Emily took a step back at his outburst, then tugged at her sweater. ''Well, now we're getting somewhere. That's a perfectly human emotion. I'm terrified myself, as you'll have noticed I've mentioned more times than necessary tonight. Next.''

''What?''

His confusion was endearing. ''Next problem or comment or gripe. I'm fairly tired and I need a bed, and I'm hoping to persuade you to let me have one of yours—just for a couple of months.''

''How about a question?''

She shrugged. She really was tired. ''Questions are acceptable.''

''Will you marry me?''

Emily sat right down on the stone hearth. Blue jumped up from where he'd been lying and came to see about her. The part of her brain that was still functioning noted that one of his eyes were blue and the other was brown.

She absently patted the dog, then stared, dumfounded and confused, at Cheyenne.

"Um." She cleared her throat. "Maybe we should lead up to that sort of question with a little discussion." She buried her fingers in the husky's thick fur.

"You're carrying my brother's babies. They deserve to have our family's name."

"Oh." Why had she allowed her mind to take that wild leap, to jump giddily to the conclusion that Cheyenne actually wanted *her*. She must be majorly tired. "I'd already planned to put Jimmy's name on the birth certificates, so the kids will be Bodines."

"I'm glad to hear that. I would still like to honor you with marriage. You're family."

"Well, not really."

"Through the children."

"If this is about your heritage, your people, I could explain it to them so they wouldn't think you were breaching any..." She waved her hand, at a loss. "Any whatever."

"I told you. I'm Cheyenne in my heart, not necessarily in practice. This has more to do with Shotgun Ridge being a small town. I'm in a public position and I have a certain standard to maintain."

"Are you telling me it's not acceptable for people to live together here?"

"It's not acceptable for *me*. It's personal."

"This seems so drastic. I have a career, a house. I'm on the verge of landing the biggest account of my career, a coup that could earn me the vice presidency in the firm. I can't just get married.''

''You're having babies.''

''But that's only temp…orary,'' she finished. She'd gotten so used to thinking of the twins as a short-term commitment.

''Not anymore. I want to know these children, Emily. You've literally humbled me with the sacrifice you've made, proved the incredible depth of your character by coming to me, giving me the opportunity to hold and know a part of my brother.''

''Oh, stop,'' she complained. ''You're making me feel like a saint. I'm not.''

''We'll debate that later. Right now you need my help. You said so. And I'm willing and happy to give it, to share my home with you for as long as you want. But for my own honor and integrity, I need to do that within the bounds of matrimony.''

''But what about when I go back to work? Will we get a divorce? Won't that be just as much of a black mark on your reputation?''

''We'll work that out when the time comes. This is important to me, Em.''

She studied him for a long time, matching his stillness, his intensity.

Good Lord, about the time she thought she'd crested the mountain, someone came along and cranked it up even higher, extending her hike into the unknown. First the babies, now the marriage.

She hadn't bargained for either.

But she understood what was behind Cheyenne's

concerns. He'd clawed for respectability as a kid, had attained it as a man. Taking a chance on losing that, even a tiny portion of it, would be huge for a man like him.

Her sense of fairness ruled. She wanted Cheyenne to know these children. She wanted him to see Jimmy's accomplishment.

And, selfishly, this was a terrible time in her life. She was scared spitless over what was to come. She trusted Cheyenne.

Oh, she didn't know him well—that was a given. It went back to that connection thing, she supposed, that intangible understanding. She felt it in her heart. And in her gut.

As though they were soul mates.

That wild, unexpected thought caused her heart to lurch and stirred the babies into their acrobatic act. She put her hand low on her abdomen, cradling them as though to soothe, to apologize for upsetting herself and them.

Could the children feel her emotions? She didn't know. There was so much she didn't know. And no one to turn to for the answers she sought.

She'd moved through the past two weeks in a fog, stunned over the death of her loved ones, stunned over the future she now faced. Up until two weeks ago, she'd basically compartmentalized her mind with these babies in one part—ignoring them to some degree—knowing that her responsibility was only short-term, that there was an end in sight. Now it was all hitting her at once.

There'd been no time to think, to read books on parenthood, to absorb the magnitude of what she faced. She wasn't supposed to be facing it. There had been no reason to arm herself with knowledge about motherhood, no reason to prepare for responsibilities beyond the birth of the babies.

And for the first time in her life, Emily had panicked.

In the midst of her panic, Cheyenne's face had come to mind, the life vest she'd grabbed hold of in the turbulent seas that were threatening to drown her.

She was living moment to moment, thinking moment to moment. Perhaps not totally rationally. Maybe her reasons for coming to him went deeper. She didn't know. Wasn't really in any shape to know.

Cheyenne was her best hope. Just for a while, though.

She didn't want to admit that her circle of friends in Washington were mostly business associates. Career people who weren't into families and diapers and trips to the park. They dealt in spreadsheets and keeping their fingers on America's pulse, trying to second-guess the next trend and how best to exploit it. They worshiped the almighty dollar and relished the cutthroat climb up the corporate ladder.

It was a world she'd been comfortable in, successful in. Until now.

"Say, yes, Emily. Let me take care of you."

She looked at him for a long moment. He was a warrior. A protector. The woman who captured this man's heart would be lucky indeed.

She doubted she could ever be that woman.

But it wasn't what she wanted, anyway, she reminded herself. It wasn't what she was looking for.

But she *was* looking for a partner to ease the load, to share her very real fears of this new, untried venture she was stepping blindly into.

Motherhood.

And, she realized with a resigned sigh, marriage.

"Okay."

"Okay?"

She was trembling like a leaf. She could be sophisticated about the whole thing, though. "Yes. Sure."

He was looking at her as though she was somebody special. And that made her uncomfortable. She was just plain Emily, darn it all.

"So do we seal the bargain with a kiss, or what?"

Before she even thought through the flippant words, words born of nerves, Cheyenne was standing in front of her, his silver-and-turquoise belt buckle brushing her swollen stomach.

"We can."

"No! I was just kidding."

His palms cradled her cheeks as he bent forward. "I'm not."

Oh...my...gosh. "Cheyenne, uh, no...really, this isn't—"

"Yes. It is. *Really.*"

The first touch of his lips was like fire. Her heart beat so hard it hurt.

And the fire just got hotter.

Sue Civil-Brown

But a woman wanted the dark, the secret shaded areas in which everyone could

Chapter Three

With the smallest movement of his lips, the slightest angling of his head, he captured emotions as wild as a prairie fire out of control. He could feel them. Taste them.

The kiss was only meant to be a test, an acceptance of a dare.

Yet it was much, much more. He felt her response clear down to his soul, the heat, the passion…the promise. Her lips were pliant and mobile, so erotic he burned. She knew exactly what to do with her tongue—and with his.

Emily Vincent knew how to kiss.

And Cheyenne realized in a hurry that he was out of control.

And in big trouble.

He eased away, felt her lips cling for a split second more. It made him feel ten feet tall. And it made him feel like a louse. He was taking advantage.

He rested his forehead against hers, her belly holding them apart. Still, the body contact was the most seductive thing he'd ever felt.

He wasn't sex-deprived, but it had been a long time for him. And why was he thinking about sex after only one kiss?

Nearly nine months pregnant—with twins, no less—and the woman still turned him on. But she wasn't a woman he could allow himself to fall for. In fact, she was the exact type he made it a point to steer clear of.

He had plenty of experience with career women. He'd been engaged to one. Beautiful, ambitious. A woman who'd said yes to matrimony in the heat of passion and dumped him in the light of day, wanting more than a small-town sheriff could offer.

From then on, he'd been careful and selective in his partners, entering only into short-term relationships where they both understood the rules.

Women were intrigued by his body and looks, turned on—but that was it. Gauging a woman's passions had never been his problem.

Getting them to stay or commit had been.

But now he found himself in a situation where *he* was the one who didn't know the rules. He might just be in over his head.

He could handle it, he told himself. They were doing this for the babies.

And for Emily.

She gave so much of herself to others. She deserved reciprocation.

As his wife, she would be respected. Accepted. Provided for.

The people of Shotgun Ridge were generally nonjudgmental, but the dynamics of the town were changing. He knew only too well how one insensitive comment could etch scars on a person's heart, make that person feel unworthy.

Then there were his own beliefs. His people were warriors. They didn't turn their backs on their own. But they were also big on honor and the revering of women. The elders in his mother's tribe—the ones who still kept a very close familial eye on his life— would never approve of Emily and him living together unless they were husband and wife. He'd told her he didn't necessarily practice the Cheyenne ways, but that wasn't exactly truthful.

He *did* endeavor to be a man of honor.

And he *did* care deeply about the opinions of his mother's people. Living an exemplary, honorable life was part of his atonement for some of the disgraces in his past.

Oh, boy. This could get interesting.

Especially since so many of his memories and fantasies were wrapped up in the very pregnant woman staring wide-eyed at him, her lips still moist from his kiss.

"We…um, probably shouldn't have done that," she whispered.

Although his heart was beating like a ceremonial drum, he found that he could laugh at how she'd managed to sound both prim and aroused. Chastising and encouraging.

"Probably not. But it felt pretty good."

Emily sighed and stepped out of his arms. She

didn't know what to do with her hands, so she smoothed them over her hair, adjusted her sweater hem. ''That's not, uh, what this marriage thing is about, right? I mean, we don't want to give either of us the wrong impression....'' He was watching her in that way of his that made her toes curl. ''Jump in anytime and help me out here,'' she said.

''I apologize.''

''You apologize?''

''I shouldn't have taken advantage.''

''Well, I wouldn't go that far. In case you weren't paying attention, I participated, as well.''

''I was paying attention.''

The softness of his voice, the intensity of his eyes, made her heart lurch. ''Um, I'm glad to hear it.'' She was a little flustered and determined not to show it. ''Can you keep a secret?''

''I've been known to, yes.''

''I've actually wanted to do that for quite a few years.''

''Kiss?''

''Kiss *you*.''

She'd thought her admission would make him smile. It was a sophisticated, perfectly mature thing to say, a tension breaker.

Instead, he frowned. ''Why?''

''Why? Have you looked in the mirror lately?'' The man was gorgeous. And exciting.

He shrugged and reached for the poker to stir the fire.

''That was a compliment, Cheyenne.''

"Thank you."

Well, that was flat as all get-out. His shoulders were stiff and she wondered if she'd made him angry. "Did I offend you?"

He turned to her and his features softened. "My looks have often been a double-edged sword. They've branded me a half-breed Indian as a kid, and a sex trophy as a man."

"Good grief. This is the twenty-first century. Mixed cultures are no big deal."

"Now they're not. Twenty-five years ago they were."

"And it still bothers you?"

"No."

"Then it must be the sex-trophy thing. I assure you," she said with a certain amount of vehemence, "I'm hardly looking for one of those!" Frankly it amazed the heck out of her that she'd even inspired that flash of lust in him in the first place. She looked like she'd swallowed a beach ball. Huge and swollen.

He grinned, his features at last relaxed. Lord, the man truly was delicious-looking. Dark and dangerous and thrilling. And gentle. An odd description to toss in among the others, but it was there. And the combination was nothing less than soul stealing.

"So what did you think?"

"Think?" Dear heaven, she was turning into a parrot. But when he looked at her that way, her brain was rendered numb. And the man changed moods faster than a designer could change the color and font on an advertising brochure. It was hard to keep up.

"About the kiss. Was it worth the wait?"

"I don't think we should be having this conversation."

"You started it."

"Yes, and you said you could keep a secret."

His brows winged up. "But it's not a secret anymore—especially seeing as it's between the two of us."

"Yes, well…" She smiled. "It was pretty good."

He shouted with laughter. "Man, trouble, if that's not a challenge, I don't know what is."

She held up her hand like a traffic cop. "This is getting out of hand. No challenge. I promise. We're two adults here. We shared a hot kiss—"

"So now it's gone from pretty good to hot."

"Are you looking for a performance rating?"

He chuckled again. "Hell if I know. Should we change the subject?"

"We should, but I have a bit more to say on the, um, subject." She ignored the amused indulgence in his eyes, because it made her feel things deep inside that she had no business feeling. "We're adults. I think we can live perfectly fine under the same roof without having to worry about kissing each other."

"Are you worried about it?"

"Well, once you do something, you usually think about doing it again. Expect it, you know. I mean, I wouldn't want us both to end up walking on eggshells or for you to think I expected something, just because we're living together—"

"Married."

"Yes. Married." She sighed. She was digging her-self a deeper hole, making it sound like this really was a big deal. It wasn't. *Liar.* "So, when do you want to do it?"

Oh, brother. That didn't come out right.

His gazed dipped to her stomach, back to her eyes. She could almost hear his thoughts—or were they her own?

Do it as in sex, kissing or marriage?

It had been many years since she'd experienced this particular phenomenon—being in the wrong place at the wrong time; *saying* the wrong thing at the wrong time.

She was a professional woman. Talking to people was part of her job. She was good at it, articulate, classy, smart.

And around Cheyenne Bodine, she went completely stupid.

"How about day after tomorrow? Gives you a day to settle in, unpack, get your bearings. I'll set it up with the courthouse—unless you want to book the church?"

"Oh, no. That doesn't seem right somehow." Sud-denly doubts swamped her. "Cheyenne, are we doing the right thing? I mean, I don't want to mess up your life, put pressure on you with your peers over having a woman living with you, but are you sure?"

"We're going to be these children's parents. Call me old-fashioned, a product of my heritage, whatever, but I believe in the sanctity of marriage when children are brought into the world." He tipped her face up with a finger under her chin. "It's important to me, Emily."

Oh, when he said it like that, when he looked at her like that, she couldn't refuse. She was a soft touch. She felt too deeply, worried too much about others.

But there was no help for it.

Cheyenne Bodine needed something from her.

And she was going to give it. Even if she didn't completely understand the rules or the depth of the need.

It was the same character trait, or fault—one of them, at least—that had brought her here in the first place.

To let Cheyenne hold Jimmy's children in his arms. To absorb his brother's essence into his heart. To heal a wound through a miracle of the blood ties that would bind him to these babies. Bind him to Jimmy. Even after Jimmy's untimely death.

And if she was perfectly honest, being alone in the pregnancy, facing the future she now faced, changed the dynamics of how she felt.

She'd always thought if she was ever to have children—and that was a very big *if* because she'd never planned to have her own—she'd only do it if she was married.

Being a married woman—even a divorced woman—would make her life easier. It was difficult to put her finger on how she actually felt. She didn't fully understand her own thought process. She was projecting herself into the future, worried about what she would *tell* people. Not that it was anybody else's business, but people were bound to ask about her marital status, her family life, the father of her children.

In her case, the explanation—if she chose to give one—would be a long and tangled one.

The kids deserved normalcy, deserved to fit in. Surrogacy and in vitro fertilization would likely set them apart and cause problems. When they went to school and the other kids asked about their parents, their daddy, it would be much easier on them to say that their mom and dad were divorced, but that both were still a big part of their lives.

And that raised even more questions.

What would they do when it was time for her to go back to work? How often would Cheyenne make the trip to Seattle? Or would he even make it?

But she wasn't going to get herself in a dither about all that now. She desperately needed Cheyenne's help.

But she would not compromise his standing in the community—or with his mother's people—to get it.

IF EMILY HAD THOUGHT her life had been turned upside down before, now it was in absolute turmoil. She'd been part of the corporate world for so long, entering into relationships that were mainly surface, business.

The people of Shotgun Ridge were as far from surface as they could get. They clucked and clapped and were downright tickled over the wedding.

"I thought you said this was going to be a *simple* thing," Emily whispered to Cheyenne. "Did you invite the whole world?'' They'd only asked Ozzie Peyton and Iris Brewer to stand up for them.

Yet the courthouse was crammed with people.

Cheyenne looked almost as uncomfortable as she felt. "I'd like to say I'm as surprised as you are, but I'm not. I've seen this happen before. Best way to handle it is just go with it."

Emily took a breath. "I hope I don't do something stupid."

Cheyenne tipped up her chin, gazed down at her. "You've never done anything stupid."

"Not intentionally. But when I lived here, something always seemed to happen, you know? I turn into a jinx. Unexpected things pop up when I least expect them." Like finding herself getting married.

"You're not a jinx."

She shrugged. "Let's just hope my water doesn't break all over the floor."

A horrified look crossed his face. "Is that a possibility? I thought you said—"

She reached up and took his hand, easing him with a smile. "I was teasing. The babies really aren't due for another three weeks. And I should know, since I was there when the little acrobats took root, so to speak."

He nodded, but still didn't look wholly convinced. "You're feeling all right, then?"

"If you don't count being overwhelmed, I'm fine."

"Brace yourself," he said softly. "I think the crowd's been as patient as they're going to be. Ozzie Peyton headed our way at four o'clock. If I forget to introduce you to someone, give me a poke in the ribs.''

''Nothing more I love than a wedding, you bet.'' Ozzie Peyton shook Cheyenne's hand, then turned to Emily. ''Well, let's have a look-see at you. You've grown up right pretty, you bet.''

''And grown *out,*'' she muttered.

Ozzie laughed, his vivid blue eyes twinkling. ''Babies are a joy and we've got ourselves a passel of them lately. Mighty fine thing you're doin' here.'' His eyes softened as they touched on her pregnant stomach. ''You have our deepest sympathies on the passing of your sister and Jimmy.''

''Thank you,'' Emily said softly, her throat aching suddenly. Debbie had been Emily's one true friend, and she missed her sister terribly. This was her wedding day. Debbie should have been standing here beside her, holding her hand, laughing and crying and teasing and offering her a tissue.

''Well, now. Didn't mean to make you sad.''

''No. It's all right. I'm fine.''

Ozzie nodded. ''I'll just go get me a good ringside seat before the other old farts get the choice ones. You bet.''

When Ozzie moved off, Cheyenne put his arm around her, held her close. His hand slipped up to her neck, beneath her hair. ''You okay?''

She nodded, looked up at him. He had lost a loved one, too. ''Are you?''

Booming laughter drew their attention. Emily felt

Cheyenne's hand tighten at her shoulder. "The preacher," he said.

Emily's heart thumped. "I thought you said this was just a justice-of-the-peace thing."

"Evidently I got overruled." He released her and shook hands with the preacher. "Emily Vincent, meet Dan Lucas."

It took a moment for Emily to find her tongue. The pastor was handsome as sin, with a smile that lit up the room and spontaneous laughter that invited everyone to share.

"I remember you," she said to Dan. "Excuse my manners, but I'd have never dreamed you'd become a minister."

Dan laughed. "Ah, you're remembering my wild and crazy days as a youth, I'm sure. We all go through our trials—schooldays were mine. And my folks'." He laughed again. "Of course with my dad and brothers all in the ministry, I always knew I'd settle down and follow."

"Well...uh, congratulations." Was that the appropriate thing to say?

More laugher. And Emily was drawn right into it, feeling relaxed and wondering how in the world that had happened. This was the *least* relaxing step she'd ever taken.

"I'm starting to get a complex, with folks trying to slip off and let Judge Lester join their lives," Dan said. "Especially since our respective sanctuaries are right next door to each other. Not that I begrudge him the chance to perform the happy duties, you understand."

A tall cowboy with a faint scar running along the side of his face stopped next to them.

"The day you get a complex is the day my horses are going to quit speaking." He had a gentle, soft-spoken voice, and in his arms he held an infant swaddled in a pink blanket, the child looking incredibly small in his big arms.

Emily was confused. "Don't you mean *start* speaking?"

"Stony's a horse whisperer," Cheyenne explained. "In his case, those horses *do* speak to him. Emily Vincent, meet Stony Stratton. The pretty ladies beside him are his wife, Eden, and their daughter, Nikki."

Eden smiled. "Welcome, Emily."

Nikki, holding a bouquet of flowers, looked up. "Can I be the flower girl? I'm real good at it. I did it three times, now—for Hannah, Dora and my mommy, Eden."

The girl, about six, Emily guessed, was precious. "Uh, sure. If you'd like. I had no idea this was going to turn into a wedding... I mean." She stopped, not sure how to proceed. Why did she continually get so tongue-tied? She was as huge as a potbelly stove, and her pale-blue maternity sweater and gray wool skirt were far from wedding fare. When she'd packed her clothes and made her decision to seek out Cheyenne, she'd hadn't realized she'd be attending one.

Especially as the bride.

Eden Stratton laid a hand on Emily's arm. "You look beautiful. I'm sorry if we've overwhelmed you." She laughed softly, her strong Southern accent lending an extra air of friendliness to her voice. "I've been in your place myself. But there's no stopping the wonderful people in this town, so just enjoy."

"I'll try. I feel…" Her words trailed off. She didn't really know *how* she felt. Like a fraud. Conspicuous. Scared silly.

"I know," Eden said, and Emily realized that she did. It was in the gentleness of her voice, the openness of her eyes. Woman-to-woman communication. "Who's standing up for you?"

"Iris Brewer."

"Here I am," Iris said, hurrying into the courthouse. "I'm so sorry I'm late. Land sakes, I had a fire to put out. Literally. It was only on the grill at the saloon, but—" Her hurried words broke off as she put her hands on Emily's shoulders, held her at arm's length. "Oh, you're positively glowing. Pregnancy does that to a woman."

In a motherly fashion, Iris drew Emily into an embrace that caused a plethora of emotions to lodge in Emily's throat.

"Thank you for asking me to stand up for you, hon. It's been a lot of years since you've seen me, and I probably seem like a stranger to you, but we'll fix that right quick, shall we?" She hugged harder, infusing Emily with acceptance and love.

"Thank *you,*" Emily whispered, swallowing hard. She nearly lost her battle with her unpredictable emotions when Iris gave an extra squeeze in understanding and compassion.

When they'd spoken on the phone yesterday, Iris

had asked about Emily's parents, whom she'd known from the days the Vincents lived in Shotgun Ridge.

Emily hadn't been able to bring herself to admit the truth. That her dad wasn't in the picture and that her mother simply wasn't interested in her life. So she'd fibbed a bit and said that there wasn't time for her mom to get here.

And Iris had promptly clucked like a mother hen and lovingly stepped in.

"Well, let's get this show on the road, shall we?" the pastor said. "Now that we've got the best man and matron of honor, we can get to it. Time enough to introduce you around after the ceremony."

Despite Pastor Dan's efforts to move them along, Emily ended up being introduced to most of her impromptu guests, her head spinning with all the new names and faces. Some she recognized from high school, some she didn't.

She met Wyatt and Hannah Malone and their children, five-year-old Ian, and one-year-old Meredith. Then Ethan and Dora Callahan and their children, two-year-old Katie and three-month-old Ryan. Ethan's two brothers—who didn't have wives or children, saving Emily from having to remember even *more* names— were there, also.

It appeared as though the entire town had taken the day off in honor of Cheyenne Bodine's marriage to a very pregnant Emily Vincent.

She might have thought it was morbid curiosity that drew them, but the community spirit and friendship was clearly evident. These people cared deeply about Cheyenne.

Oh, dear Lord, what had she gotten them both into? Was she being selfish? She would go back to Washington in a few months, but these people were his family. What would that do to his life?

"Emily?"

She jerked, realized someone had just asked her a question.

The preacher.

"Do you take Cheyenne as your lawfully wedded husband?"

She wanted to say, "Wait a minute, I need to think."

She opened her mouth. "Yes." Her heart lurched so hard she felt faint. She wasn't going to back out, to humiliate him. He was her rescuer. He'd been deprived of his family, of Jimmy, through pride and a fault that was shared equally between brothers.

She meant to see that painful gap mended.

Cheyenne and Jimmy both deserved this reunion of family—even if Jimmy wasn't here in person to reap the benefits.

Because this town was all about family.

She looked into Cheyenne's eyes, saw his questions, his own reserve, his gentle compassion. This man had depths she doubted she could ever touch.

"I do," she repeated.

Lost in his bottomless, obsidian eyes, the rest of the ceremonial exchange had a surreal feel to it, as though Emily were outside herself watching two very opposite people vow to love, honor and cherish, all the while their gazes clinging, their thoughts hidden.

And when at last Dan Lucas announced that Cheyenne Bodine should kiss his new bride, it seemed the most natural thing in the world to lean into him, to raise up on tiptoe, her hand against his chest, his large palms cupping her face, and to seal the bargain with a traditional kiss.

But nothing about this whole day felt traditional.

An instant before his lips touched hers, his intense eyes asked a silent question. *Okay?*

And with her own eyes, she answered, *Yes. Thank you for asking. Thank you for taking care of me, for taking care with me. Thank you for not letting me go through this alone.*

Applause broke into her consciousness.

The kiss and her emotions made her giddy. She swayed, and Cheyenne's arms were right there to steady her, his sharp gaze examining, assessing.

Her new husband watched her like a hawk.

A protector.

It was much more than the star he wore on his chest, more than the civil oath he'd sworn to the people to protect and serve, more than the vow he'd just made to honor and cherish in sickness and in health.

After that soul-stirring, gentle and all-too-brief kiss, it was much, much more.

He was special. And he made her feel special.

And she told herself to just hold it right there, to stop getting carried away.

Although it felt like a fairy tale, this wasn't for keeps.

Chapter Four

"Where are we going?" Instead of heading back to his truck after the ceremony, Cheyenne steered her across the street.

"The doctor's office."

"Cheyenne, I'm fine. Just tired. I don't need to go to the doctor. Besides, we don't have an appointment."

"We don't need one."

Short of trying to tug him to a halt, which she didn't think she could do, she let him sweep her along. She glanced around to see if people noticed where they were going, but most of the guests had already left, excusing themselves to get their cranky children home and see to their livestock.

Cheyenne's uncle, John White Cloud, who'd silently slipped into the church and stood at the back apart from everyone else, had also left. Emily wanted to ask why the man hadn't spoken to them, but right now it was all she could do to keep up.

"I don't remember this pushy side of you. You might *ask* instead of steamrollering ahead."

"You've been rubbing your back most of the day and you nearly fainted after the ceremony."

Well, good grief. Who wouldn't swoon after kissing Cheyenne Bodine?

"I'm fine," she repeated, and smoothed a hand over her stomach. "There're two babies in here. It's a bit of a load to carry around."

"Humor me."

Since he was carefully propelling her with a protective arm around her back, she had little choice but to comply. It was probably a good idea, anyway. She'd seen her own doctor just before she'd left Seattle and gotten a list of ob-gyn's who practiced in both Miles City and Billings, but it wouldn't hurt to get acquainted with the doctor here.

Still, this was her wedding day, crazy as that seemed. And here she was, on her way to let another man—other than her new husband—examine her body.

Good grief, what a thought. Pregnancy was obviously affecting her brain.

They paused in front of the clinic, and Emily noticed that mere feet separated this door from the veterinarian's office. It'd be just her luck to wander in the wrong door one day.

"Do patients ever get confused and end up at the wrong specialist's office?"

Cheyenne grinned down at her, his black hat tipped low over his brow. "I'm not sure. I've known instances where one doc was unavailable and the other was called as backup."

"The vet to deliver babies and the medical doctor to deliver animals?" She laughed. "That doesn't surprise me. If I was in an emergency situation, I'd go for anybody with *any* kind of medical know-how."

"Even me?"

"You have a medical background?"

"EMT training. I delivered a baby by the side of the highway once."

She felt the warmth of his body next to hers, supportive, comforting…capable. And suddenly she was very glad that he was in her life. "You're a handy man to have around, Bodine."

"Glad you approve…Bodine."

Her heart fluttered. Yes, she was a Bodine now. And she'd keep the name, she decided. She and the babies would have the same last name. It would make it so much easier when filling out school forms or enrolling them in preschool.

Lord, there were so many things to think about. And they all scared her to death.

Cheyenne opened the door and she went in ahead of him, stepping aside as a family of four went out.

A young woman in a nurse's uniform looked up quickly from the chart she was reading.

"Hey, Kelly," Cheyenne said. "Is the doc in?"

"Yes. Just finished up with his last patient." She glanced at Emily's swollen stomach. "Are you in labor, or just darn close?"

"Darn close—I hope," Emily said. "Three more weeks to go, and believe me, I'm ready." Ready to get rid of the discomfort. Not necessarily ready for what would follow.

"I hear you. The last few weeks are the toughest. At least we're past the hot season." She glanced at Emily's ankles, obviously looking for swelling. "Did you want to see the doctor?"

"If it's not a good time—"

"Yes, we do," Cheyenne interrupted.

Emily raised a brow at his high-handed, brook-no-argument tone, and the nurse laughed.

"I'm Kelly Anderson," she said. "Dr. Hammond's assistant. And you are?"

"My wife, Emily," Cheyenne answered before Emily could even get her mouth open. She glared again, but he simply ignored her. They were going to have to speak about this bossy, steamrollering penchant of his.

"Oh! Congratulations. I didn't know you'd gotten married."

"Just now, in fact."

"Well, come on back and I'll let the doctor know you're here."

Emily started to follow, then frowned when Cheyenne trailed right behind her. "I can do this by myself."

"But you don't need to now." His unreadable gaze skimmed her hair, her lips, her stomach.

"I'm *not* taking my clothes off in front of you," she whispered vehemently.

His grin put her in mind of what the wolf might

have looked like gazing at Little Red Riding Hood. "Don't recall asking you to."

She sighed and continued walking. Of course he wouldn't ask her to. She was as far from sex-inspiring as a woman could get. And why in the world was she thinking about sex when she was about to go into a doctor's examining room, for pity's sake?

She would be heartily glad when her wild emotions settled back down to normal. These little babies were causing more havoc than she'd ever dreamed they would.

Not listening, or at least politely ignoring them, Kelly tapped on a closed door and stuck her head in. "A patient to see you." She pushed the door wider, and Emily took one look at the doctor and felt her heart sink right down to her toes. Oh, no.

"I'll be out front if you need me," Kelly said. A silent moment passed between doctor and assistant, as though each was putting far more different connotations on the word *need.* Kelly glanced quickly away and hurried out.

Dr. Chance Hammond took a little longer to bring his attention back to the patient at hand.

Well, that was interesting, Emily thought. A little bit of tension between doctor and assistant, a whole lot of sizzle. Or was she simply seeing things, reading romance into every face because she'd just come from her own wedding?

A convenience wedding, she reminded herself.

Not a wedding based on romance and love.

Why that realization made her feel a pang, she couldn't say. Hormones, she decided.

And those haywire emotions were going down another path at the moment, dragging her along faster than she could keep up.

Had *all* the men in this town grown up to be absolute hunks?

"Hey, Chance. This is Emily Vincent—Bodine now. We just got married."

"I know. I'd have been there, but the Jeffersons came in at the last minute. One of the kids decided to share the flu with the rest of the family. How are you, Emily? And congratulations."

"I'm fine. And thank you. And you're *not* examining me!" Oh, Lord, how had that slipped out?

Chance frowned. Rather than looking at Cheyenne for an explanation, which she appreciated, he kept his professionally assessing gaze on her. "Is there a problem?"

Emily sighed and ran a nervous hand through her hair. "I'm sorry. That came out wrong. But good grief, I knew you in school. I'm…this is beyond embarrassing."

"You're having a baby, Emily—"

"Babies," she corrected.

"Twins?" At her nod, he continued. "All the more reason you need medical monitoring. Acquaintance or not, when it comes to medicine, there is no place for, or any thoughts along, an unprofessional line. I assure you, my ethics are beyond reproach."

"I know. I'm sure they are. I'm just…I don't know.

I feel weird. I had a checkup last week, so I really don't need an examination, and… I'm making a hash of this. I'm sorry. I don't want to offend you.'' It seemed like all she'd done since she'd gotten to Shotgun Ridge was apologize.

He gently motioned her into a chair, glanced at Cheyenne and indicated he should sit, also. ''Okay. I understand.''

''You do?'' She felt like an idiot.

Chance nodded. ''If you'll be more comfortable, Kelly can handle the basics of your care if you don't want to make the trek into the city every week. How far along are you?''

''Due in three weeks.''

''Mmm. Time to keep a pretty close eye. Were you planning to deliver in Billings or Miles City?''

''In either one. I have some referrals.''

''I'll have a look and add my own to it. Margo Freeman's an excellent ob-gyn at Holy Rosary Hospital in Miles City.'' He pressed an intercom button on the phone. ''Kelly, would you come back in here, please?'' To Emily he said, ''In the meantime, would it be okay if I just took a little history from you?''

''Yes. I don't know why I acted so strongly.''

''No problem. I'd be a little edgy, too. After all, it was my fault you got hauled off to jail by Sheriff Conroy.''

Cheyenne looked at Emily, his dark eyes filled with amusement and curiosity. ''I don't think I heard about that one.''

She sighed. ''It was purely a case of overreaction—

although Chance was the one doing the reckless driving. I was minding my own business in the back of his pickup with a bunch of other girls.''

''And you forgot to tell me you were underage,'' Chance said in his own defense.

''You never asked. And I didn't know you were going to take a shortcut and leave tire tracks all through Langley's wheat field.'' It was that jinx thing again, Emily thought. Out of everyone, *she* was the one whose parents had been summoned to come pick her up at the sheriff's office. And by the next day the story had been so distorted, everyone had thought *she* had been driving the pickup. How the tale had included her mowing down Langley's prize rooster was still a mystery to her.

The reminiscing broke the ice, and by the time Kelly Anderson came into the office, Emily was feeling much more relaxed.

Even though Chance Hammond had put aside reckless behavior in favor of saving lives and healing the sick, she was still glad that there was a woman available to turn to.

''Pull up a chair, Kelly,'' Chance said. ''Emily's about three weeks from term in her pregnancy. I'm going to refer her to an ob-gyn, but we'll get a chart started, anyway.'' When the assistant was seated, Chance looked back at Emily. ''Any problems we should be aware of?''

''No. Although the doctors told me multiple births are considered high-risk pregnancies, I've pretty much sailed through.'' She could feel Cheyenne watching her, obviously leaving it up to her whether or not she wanted to explain the circumstances of the pregnancy. "I'm, uh, actually a surrogate."

To his credit, Chance didn't even bat an eye. Neither did Kelly, though there were plenty of questions in their eyes. She told them about the in vitro fertilization using Debbie's egg and Jimmy's sperm. It took a while to get it all sorted out, to explain about Jimmy and Debbie, to accept condolences and experience the raw pain all over again, the pain that continually lurked, but that she'd managed to subdue.

And through it all, Chance Hammond gave her his full attention, his demeanor professional and friendly. The only time he really reacted was when Cheyenne leaned in close to her, reached for her hand, lending his own comfort, sharing her hurt and grief, infusing her with his strength.

It was the type of thing a husband or lover would do.

Cheyenne and Chance were friends. The doctor was obviously speculating about the undercurrents here, wondering if there was a history, if there was more.

Cheyenne was her husband. As for the lover part…well, a girl couldn't have it all. And why in the world was she even thinking along those lines?

It was those kisses, she decided. She'd have to make sure that sort of thing didn't continue.

Her emotions were already strung out enough.

WHEN THEY GOT HOME, Cheyenne went out and worked with the horses. He needed time to clear his head. Getting married and going to his new wife's first doctor's appointment was a little too surreal for comfort.

For about the thousandth time, he questioned his sanity, wondered why he'd pushed for marriage.

The sound of a truck pulling up in front of the barn usually didn't faze him.

But he knew the sound of this particular truck. A diesel engine. On the Ford his uncle drove.

He gave Thunder's cheek a scratch, set down the currycomb and went to the door of the barn, watching as his uncle John climbed out of the truck.

The older man's steel-gray hair was a couple of inches past his shoulders, tied at the nape with a strip of leather. Normally whiskers covered his lower chin, but he'd shaved—evidently in honor of the wedding.

Which he'd barely stayed for.

"Uncle," Cheyenne said, holding out his hand in greeting. "I figured you'd stop by."

"I brought Martin."

Cheyenne nodded at his young cousin, who shrugged as if to say, "Don't ask me nothing. You know the old man." Martin, who was seventeen and Cheyenne's main source of help at the ranch, had his own vehicle. He didn't need to bum rides from their uncle.

"Any problems I need to know about?" Martin asked.

When Cheyenne shook his head, the kid went into the barn. He knew his way around this ranch as well as Cheyenne did.

So did John, for that matter. John White Cloud had always taken an interest in Cheyenne's life, and he came out to the ranch often. He was a man of few words, but his silence often spoke volumes.

"So, Uncle, why didn't you stay and meet Emily?"

"We have met."

"When she was young."

"Yes. And now she is carrying my great-nephew."

"Maybe a niece. Or one of each." Although what that had to do with meeting her now, Cheyenne had no idea.

John nodded and moved with Cheyenne into the barn. Picking up a pitchfork, he automatically began shifting straw in one of the stalls. Cheyenne grabbed another tool and worked alongside him, knowing the man would say what he wanted in his own time.

"She has the look of class about her."

"Mmm. She's a bigwig at an advertising agency. Jimmy worked for them, too."

"Jimmy had a fine talent for art. I imagine he did well at his work."

"Emily said he did."

John worked in silence for several minutes, his big weathered hands gripping the handle of the pitchfork as he hefted straw and spread it around the stall. Age hadn't slowed him down at all.

"This is a good thing she has done for our Jimmy."

"Yes." The familiar smell of horses and hay and leather soothed him, which was a wonder since his gut had been clenched and jumping for days now. Ever since Emily Vincent—Bodine—had let herself into his house and his life and fallen asleep in his bed like a modern-day Goldilocks.

"A woman who sacrifices, who loves this deeply, is special. You have done the right thing by offering marriage."

"Have I?"

John's fork paused for just an instant. "You are a man of honor, Nephew. You have made the family proud."

Cheyenne sighed and leaned against the pitchfork, abandoning his chore for the moment. Martin was measuring feed and checking the mares they would soon breed. Mustangs were a species whose bloodlines had degenerated over the years. Cheyenne's goal was to strengthen those bloodlines by breeding them with Thoroughbreds with barb ancestry. Ethan Callahan and his brothers helped out with the breeding, Cheyenne raised the animals and Stony Stratton trained them. With the combined efforts, his mustang stock was becoming some of the finest in the land.

And that, too, made the family proud.

"Emily's concerned that she's out of her element with the babies. She came only to get my help for a few months."

"Yet you wonder if it will last past *Hoats en shi.*"

The Hoop Moon, Cheyenne translated mentally. January. It wasn't a question. His uncle had visions, yet was mysterious about them. He often spoke in riddles, would drop a bombshell, yet make recipients figure out the meaning on their own.

Did he hope it would last longer?

"We have nothing in common, Uncle. She has a job in Washington."

"The children need family."

"And they'll have it. I won't try to hold her."

John stopped pushing the hay around, straightened. Like Cheyenne, he was a tall man. Proud. Wise. And when he looked at you, it was as though he could truly see inside, ferret out all your secrets.

"There is no shame in a man asking for what he needs."

Cheyenne felt his gut twist. "I have everything I need."

John studied him for a few minutes longer. Then in a move that Cheyenne was used to, he changed the subject.

"Will you still be inviting the children to come out and ride?"

"Yes. I'd like to postpone it though. Give me time to be on hand for the first few weeks that Emily will need the most help." Each month his uncle brought the children from the reservation to Cheyenne's ranch to spend a few hours riding horses, eating burgers and roasting marshmallows in the fireplace. Cheyenne looked forward to the monthly visits as much as the kids did.

"Let's make it early December. As soon as I get the Christmas lights up."

"That will be more of a treat."

There were still hardships on the reservation, although dealings with the gas and oil companies had greatly elevated their income. Cheyenne ached for some of those children, seeing himself in them.

"I should take leave so that you can get back to your new wife."

New wife. The words had his heart pounding. And for some really odd reason, he was almost afraid to go into the house.

"Why don't you come in and meet Emily?"

"As I said before, we have met. Another time I will come for a proper visit."

"There's nothing wrong with now."

"Another time. When the babies come, I'll bring gifts."

Cheyenne knew he couldn't budge his uncle once the man's mind was made up. "As you wish. You can go ahead and take Martin with you. I can finish up with the horses."

He still needed time to himself, time to come to grips with the changes today had wrought in his life. Changes he'd instigated himself.

Why did he sense that his life was slipping out of his control?

Chapter Five

They'd only been married for two days and she already had something to confess.

Emily sighed and took off her coat, tossing her car keys on the counter. The kitchen was her least favorite room in the house—not that Cheyenne's was anything to complain about. Spacious, it had all the required gadgets, was made warm and homey by maple cabinets and furniture and pale-green tile on the counters.

Her own kitchen in her Washington condo was solid white, decorated with a cherry-blossom theme. But that was pretty much the extent of her contribution to that particular room. Decorating. And keeping the cookie jar stocked with goodies.

She scooped dry dog food into Blue's dish, then gave him a French fry by way of apology. "I'll share my dinner with you later if you promise not to tell."

Blue licked her hand, then perked up his ears and whipped his head toward the doorway, his tags jingling.

Cheyenne stood there, one shoulder propped against the doorjamb, watching her. He looked incredibly sexy in his jeans and khaki uniform shirt. A sheepskin jacket hung open on his tall, muscular frame, and the brim of his black Stetson hat rode low on his brow.

Her gaze clung to him, moving from the top of his head down. Just looking at him made her forget to breathe.

Neither she nor the dog had heard him come in.

"Don't you wear a gun belt?" *Well, good one, Emily. Blurt out to the man that you were looking at the front of his pants!* Obviously lack of air had affected her brain.

"Sometimes. Not usually when I'm home, though."

"Oh." Brilliant conversationalist. She didn't know why she felt so tongue-tied all of a sudden. This was ridiculous.

He tipped his hat farther back on his head, glanced at the aluminum containers of chicken she was taking out of the oven. "I heard you made a trip to the beauty shop today."

"How?"

"Deputy saw your car. Then Arletta was talking about you over lunch at Brewer's."

"I'd forgotten how fast word travels in small towns. She wasn't saying anything bad, was she?" And if the deputy had told him about seeing her at the beauty shop, had he told him about the *other* incident?

"No. Unless you think it's bad that everyone in town knows you had your fake fingernails removed."

"They weren't fake. Merely acrylics overlaid on my own nails." Why was she defending her fingernails? "I thought it'd be smart with the babies coming and

all. I might not have time for the upkeep. But why in
the world would anybody be interested in that?''

He shrugged, his gaze dipping to her stomach. She
had an idea that he saw a lot in a single glance.

"Everybody's interested in *anything* around here.
Arletta's fairly awed by you.''

"By me? Why?''

"You're a celebrity in her book. To hear her tell it,
you practically star in the commercials you do, rub
elbows with some pretty impressive people.''

She laughed and absently smoothed her hand over
her stomach where the babies were frolicking. "It's
not as glamorous as it sounds. We just come up with
the ideas and sell them to the media buyers. I don't
mingle with the cast.''

"Arletta's pea green that you *did* actually mingle
with Mel Gibson.''

"That one was special. I actually flew out for the
taping and screening—which I usually don't do.''

"Just couldn't resist the lure of Gibson, hmm?''

"Jealous?''

"Maybe.''

She laughed. "That particular commercial was
pretty special. My main arena is print advertising, but
that idea came to me like a gift fully formed and fairly
begged for a different medium. It was solely my baby
and it aired on Super Bowl Sunday. I won a Clio
award for it.''

"Congratulations.''

"Thank you. The recognition meant a lot. And

Mel's a really great guy. Charming and hysterically funny, a real jokester.''

"Mel, huh?''

She gave him a saucy, secretive look. Like he'd really be jealous, she thought. "The guy's a committed family man, Bodine. He wouldn't look twice at someone like me.''

"Then he'd be a fool.''

His voice was so soft, his eyes so intense, she shivered. Why in the world did he say things like that to her? Use that sexy, exciting tone of voice as though she was a tempting package wrapped in a pretty bow that he was just dying to untie and get his hands on?

She tugged at the hem of her sweater, flustered, not knowing where to look or how to act.

And he still hadn't mentioned the *other* thing.

She opened the cupboards, looking for paper plates. Cheyenne reached over her head and took down two ceramic plates. The blue-and-tan Southwestern design was faded from use.

"You don't have paper ones?''

His dark eyes settled on her, and his sensual lips twitched ever so slightly. "No.''

She ignored his amusement. "I'll have to fix that. I hate to do dishes.''

"You cooked. I'll do dishes.''

"Well, I didn't actually cook.'' She transferred the chicken onto the plates, then abandoned the task and quickly wadded up the brown to-go bag with the Brewer's Saloon logo on it and tossed it into the trash.

She wasn't a domestic goddess. He'd just have to deal with it.

He was still watching her with that almost-there smile.

"Well," she said in her own defense, "the town hasn't grown any fast-food places since I left. Brewer's is it."

"Did I say anything?"

"No. And if you did, you'd be doing the cooking."

"I'll do it, anyway. I don't mind."

Oh, dear. This was starting to stack up pretty one-sided. If he was going to do the dishes and the cooking, *plus* get saddled with marriage in the bargain, not to mention babies on the way, what was he getting out of the deal?

"Have a seat, speed demon."

She'd wondered when he'd get around to bringing that up. Sighing, she noticed he'd efficiently added the coleslaw and French fries to the plates.

She eased her huge self into the chair at the kitchen table. "You heard about that, too?"

"Mm." He sat down across from her. "Deputy wrote you up for doing eighty-eight miles an hour."

"I'm sure it was only eighty-five. And I told him I was your wife."

"Mm-hmm." He bit into a French fry.

"Are you laughing?"

"Certainly not." Yet the corners of his mouth tipped. "Trying to bribe an officer of the law is serious business."

"I wasn't…" She took a breath. "I thought *every-*

one knew we'd gotten married. And I'd like to know what kind of men you're hiring these days who would threaten to haul a pregnant woman to jail.''

He chuckled. ''Boyd's new. And the way I heard it, you threatened him first.''

She took a sudden interest in the juicy chicken in front of her. ''There wasn't a speck of traffic on the road. It was ridiculous. And I was late.'' She pushed the meat around on her plate. ''Honestly, this kind of thing hardly ever happens to me.''

He raised a brow.

''Well, not since I was young, anyway. I'm sorry if I embarrassed you.''

''Do I look embarrassed?''

''No. Come to think of it, you look pretty smug. So, what's the deal? Is this going to end up on my driving record?''

''I'm the boss. I imagine I can get your ticket fixed.''

She felt her grin growing. ''You *imagine?* If I told you I got one of Eden Stratton's raspberry cheesecakes for dessert, would that tip the scales in my favor?''

''That'd probably do it. The woman bakes like a dream.''

A statement like that might have made another woman feel inadequate. Not Emily. She could cook. She just didn't particularly like to do it—nor did she usually have the time.

''Then you'll be ecstatic to know that despite the fact that cooking's not high on my résumé's list of assets, I do great takeout. And I even brought home some of her scones and caramel buns. Brewer's carries a whole line of Eden's baked goodies. Though frankly, I'll probably wish I'd never found that out. I'll be big as a barn, instead of a mere house.''

''You're not big as a house. You're pregnant and cute. And I imagine doing takeout's going to become more trouble than it's worth. Especially when the snow comes. Besides, I'm not all that keen on you running up and down the highway as it is. You look like you're ready to pop.''

Emily couldn't decide which statement or emotion to grab on to. Her mind rolled his words around. He thought she was cute. She'd have preferred beautiful, but then that was stretching honesty. Still, it made her feel warm and giddy. He'd also said she wasn't in competition with the house—sizewise—then in nearly the next breath had told her she looked ready to pop. She decided not to take offense.

As for the running-up-and-down-the-road comment, well, that was a little too bossy-sounding for comfort.

''Guess it's a good thing that I'm married to such a handy guy, isn't it? I mean, you *do* have experience delivering babies on the highway.''

He choked on a swallow of chicken, reached quickly for his glass of water, then glared at her. ''Don't even *think* that. Knowing you, it'll come to pass.''

She wondered if she should feel insulted that he was obviously thinking there was merit to this jinx thing.

The masculine horror on his handsome face was so endearing she couldn't work up a decent pique.

CHEYENNE CAME HOME the next day to find his house in utter chaos.

Well, not *utter,* but close.

"Mort," he said, nodding in greeting to the telephone-installation guy shoving tools back in his belt.

"Afternoon, Cheyenne. Just finished up. Sorry about the mess. Told the wife to give a call over to Jake McCall's office. He'll send someone out to patch up that drywall, and you'll never even know I was here."

Mort wasn't known for his perfectionism. But he knew his way around a phone system.

Not that Cheyenne was aware anything was wrong with his to begin with.

Evidently "the wife" thought differently.

"What do I owe you?"

"Got it covered. Take care of that lady of yours. She's a gem."

Yes, Cheyenne thought as Mort let himself out. Emily was definitely a gem—and more. And that was starting to worry him.

Because she wasn't really his lady. She was only temporary. Like every other woman in his life.

But she didn't *feel* like every other woman in his life. She felt special. And she turned him inside out.

He never knew what she was going to do next, which was why he felt the need to ease up on his workload and drop in at home more often.

To his consternation, she didn't seem inclined to pay his worries any heed. She should be taking it easy, yet instead, she raced up and down the road in her sporty Mercedes, visiting the beauty shop and ordering dinner to go from Brewer's Saloon…getting a speeding ticket. He'd taken some flack over that one.

He felt a grin tug and was helpless to stop it.

He was amused by her, intrigued and so turned on half the time he didn't know what to do with himself.

He was used to being alone. And sharing living quarters with Emily was taking some adjustment. Feminine things were all around. Emily was a very feminine woman. And his whole house smelled like her. Vanilla. It made him hungry. And he ought not to be thinking about that kind of hunger when she was so close to delivering.

He found her in one of the extra bedrooms she'd appropriated for office use. He recognized the scarred pine desk as one he'd stored in the garage.

He'd spent hours studying at that desk as a kid, determined to prove his intelligence, determined to show Vanessa Peyton she wasn't wasting her time on him. Ozzie Peyton's late wife had been the schoolteacher in Shotgun Ridge, and Cheyenne hadn't made her job easy. He'd been a sullen kid, a hell-raiser, but she'd straightened him right out using a firm hand and an ocean of compassion. She'd taken an interest in him, taught him to reach for his dreams.

And for that, Cheyenne owed a lot to the Peytons and to this town.

He stepped into the room, and Emily's head jerked up. She slapped a hand to her chest. "Cheyenne! You scared me half to death. I thought everyone was gone."

"They are. Busy morning?"

"Not bad. I had an extra telephone line installed."

"So I see. I didn't know we needed one."

She shrugged. "There's no need for you to foot the bill for my business expenses."

He frowned. He didn't know her financial status, but there was every possibility that she made more money than he did. Oh, he had plenty of money, had made wise investments over the years. His riches came from the land and the horses he bought and sold. His salary from the county was a good one, but he doubted it matched hers.

"I think I can afford to pay the phone bill."

"I have an expense account, Cheyenne. If I'm making business calls, the company should pay for it."

He didn't know why he'd gotten so touchy. Or maybe he did. Linda, who'd been engaged to him for all of forty-eight hours, had looked down on his ranch life and sheriff duties. He hadn't been good enough—rich enough.

He hadn't had the right address. One with a big-city zip code.

He glanced around the room at the laptop computer, portable printer, fax machine and all the papers and files scattered over the desk.

"Aren't you supposed to be on maternity leave?"

Emily straightened her papers and put them back in their files. For a minute there Cheyenne had seemed in an odd mood. There were times when he went silent and watchful, and she didn't have a clue what he was thinking. She had an idea, though, that he was worried about her. It was sweet. And it pleased her more than she wanted to admit. There weren't many people in her life who worried about her.

"A working leave. A cosmetics company I've been trying to get is on the verge of signing with us. I can't drop the ball now."

"Can't you delegate the work?"

"I have. Most of it. But I started this campaign before I knew I'd be taking care of the babies." She frowned at her own choice of words. She still said things like "taking care," as though she were baby-sitting. She hadn't gotten used to thinking in terms of the children being her sole responsibility.

Well, not hers solely anymore. Hers and Cheyenne's. But it still changed things. Negotiations with Cherie Cosmetics were fierce. Even getting a piece of their business would be major. And Emily was the one who'd made the contact. She was the one who'd sold the idea, the one they'd put their trust in. Cockran Advertising had an excellent reputation, but Emily had brought in the account.

She couldn't just abandon it now that she was so close to attaining the goal she'd worked for and sweated blood over for so long. Bagging this account would practically give her an engraved invitation for a much coveted promotion. Vice President of Cockran Advertising.

Thankfully, with a phone, fax and computer modem, it was nearly as good as being in the office.

"How'd the furniture get in here?"

She glanced around the room, pleased with how it

was shaping up. "Mort called a couple of guys to help out. I hope you don't mind that I did this."

"This is your home now. You can do what you want."

Temporary home, she thought, and chastised herself for the pang that settled beneath her breastbone.

"So what are you doing home in the middle of the day? It's barely past lunchtime."

"I thought we could go into the city and shop for baby furniture."

"That's a great idea," she said. "We can clock how long it takes to get to the hospital while we're at it."

"I've got a fairly good idea about that."

"I'd feel better if I knew it firsthand."

"Like to be in control, hmm?"

"It's not a crime."

"No. It's not. We can do that. Are you sure you're up to it, though? Looks like you've already put in a full day."

He was worried again. She wanted to hug him. Resisted. "I'm not an invalid, Cheyenne. I'm just pregnant."

"And stubborn. Get your coat, trouble. It's turning cold."

CHEYENNE USHERED EMILY into a café in Miles City for an early dinner, watching her like a hawk, holding her chair, taking her coat. It was so sweet—though she didn't dare say that. She'd already said that once today, and he'd scowled at her as though she'd maligned his masculinity.

But he *was*—sweet and sexy and worrying like a grizzly over a cub—which he would vehemently deny if she pointed it out. He projected a tough-guy image to the world. Emily saw right past it.

She'd told him she was fine so many times during the day she wasn't going to say that again, either.

"I can't wait to get all that furniture delivered," she said, taking a sip of water and making a dive for the breadbasket.

"Yeah, I think we figured that out when you insisted it had to be today."

"Well, you told me Gerard's a friend of yours and lives close by. And he said he didn't mind taking the delivery truck home."

Cheyenne just smiled at her. "When you decide to do something, you don't mess around, do you?"

She could say the same about him. He'd proposed marriage and had the ceremony completed within two days of her arrival.

And talk about stubborn. They'd had a bit of a scuffle over who would pay for the nursery items. Cheyenne had pointed out that this wasn't an expense-account item. He'd won the argument by sheer force of his personality—and the fact that his name was on the deed to the house the furniture was going into.

Emily smiled. "I think Gerard was secretly afraid I'd have the babies before we could get a crib for them to sleep in."

He glanced at her stomach, which was pressing against the table of the booth. "If I didn't know your due date, I'd worry, too."

He was worried, anyway. She could tell.

The waitress delivered their orders, and although Emily was ravenous, she wasn't sure there was a whole lot of room inside her to put food. With her stomach wedged against the table, she couldn't find a comfortable position.

"You haven't said much about your folks, other than telling Iris your mom couldn't make it to the wedding."

Emily pushed at the pasta she'd hardly made a dent in, then laid down her fork. "That was a little bit of a fib."

He raised a brow, waited to see if she'd continue.

She sighed. "My folks divorced about a year after we left Shotgun Ridge."

"I'm sorry."

Shrugging, she said, "It was for the best. They didn't get along, and at the end it was as though they hated each other. Mom was selling real estate and Dad was having an affair. The divorce was pretty ugly. Mom became a workaholic and Dad disappeared. I'm still not sure where he is."

"Is your mother still in Washington?"

The underlying question she heard was, why hadn't Emily turned to Tamara to help out with the babies?

"No. She moved to Maine and remarried. We don't stay in contact. Mom has her own life now and she makes no secret that she's concentrating on herself. She feels she gave away her best years to the family and now it's her turn."

Emily understood her mom's need to put herself

first, but Tamara had gone to the extreme end of the scale. Her life revolved around her job, her new marriage and her husband's healthy bank account.

There was no middle ground, no compromise, no obvious maternal feelings for the two daughters she'd left behind. It was as though once Emily and Debbie were grown, Tamara felt she'd done her duty and didn't need to do any more.

"What about the babies? They're her grandchildren."

"It's hard to explain my mother. She's so different now. Selfish. In some ways that's good, and I support her right to be her own woman, but in others...well, she just didn't understand why I would take a chance on jeopardizing my job by agreeing to be a surrogate in the first place, or why Debbie was so desperate for children of her own—or why I was keeping the kids now that Debbie's gone."

"Sounds more insensitive than selfish, if you ask me."

"Like I said, once Mom washed her hands of her old life, her philosophy on just about everything did a complete one-eighty. I can't change her, so I don't try."

"Did she even come to the funeral?"

"Yes. Flew in and out the same day."

He reached for her hand. She turned her palm up and linked her fingers with his, grateful for the compassion. She tried not to think about her mother's actions, how they hurt. How she'd felt when her mother had told her she wasn't staying, that she didn't have any advice to give about the motherless babies Emily carried, didn't have time in her life to offer help.

Just as Emily hadn't considered herself these children's mother, Tamara hadn't given much thought to her role as a grandmother, other than perhaps sending a birthday card or holiday gift once or twice a year.

And that was when it had hit home to Emily that she was totally alone, without anyone who truly cared to help her out, to see her through the rough times. She hadn't realized how desperately she'd wanted her mother to take her in her arms, to tell her it would all work out fine, that they were a family, and that Emily could count on that bond, that they'd put their heads together and figure out something.

Tamara hadn't even asked Emily to drive her to the airport. She'd simply had a cab waiting, left Emily numb, alone with her sorrow and the quicksand in which her life had sunk.

Alone with her panic.

"I have to believe that in her own way, my mother does love me. And she's grieving for Debbie, too, but she's afraid to show it. Maybe the babies were just too painful a reminder." She absently stroked her thumb over the back of his hand. "I know it all sounds pretty horrible, but I don't want you to hold it against her. I'm still hoping she'll come around someday, get to know her grandchildren." But right now she wasn't willing, didn't have time, hadn't scheduled it into her plans to help out.

So Emily had been left on her own.

Except for Cheyenne.

He astonished her by lifting their linked hands to his lips, brushing a kiss across her knuckles. His gaze held hers, his eyes intense, filled with thoughts and emotions she couldn't read.

"Do you know how rare you are?"

"To have a dysfunctional family?"

He shook his head. "To have such a compassionate, good heart."

"Now don't go putting me on some pedestal. I was plenty upset over the whole ordeal. But I know what it's like to concentrate on a career."

"You don't see it, do you?" he asked softly.

"What?"

He shook his head, pressed his lips once more to her knuckles, squeezed and let go. "You want everyone to think you're this tough-as-nails executive, that the incredible things you do, the sacrifices you make for everyone else, are no big deal. Yet *you* are a very big deal." His voice went deep and soft. "I'm really proud to know you."

The timbre of his voice alone caused a lump to form in her throat. She was both touched by and uncomfortable with his praise. Because her own thoughts weren't always so unselfish.

She desperately wanted the vice presidency of Cockran Advertising. And though it would be a juggling act when the babies came, she still planned to pursue it. So she did have something in common with her mother. The drive to make it to the top.

"Um, we should probably hit the road. Gerard will beat us to the house."

His look said he knew she was discounting her qualities again, but he didn't say anything.

After he paid the bill, Cheyenne helped her out of the booth and held her white parka as she threaded her arms through the sleeves. Chills raced over her skin as he lifted her hair free of her collar, let his fingers linger.

To cover her unease, she laughed and preceded him out the door, giving up on getting the zipper closed.

"Good thing these kids won't be sticking out like this much longer. I'd have to get a new coat."

Cheyenne put his arm around her, drawing her close to his warmth. "If you're not concerned with fashion, you can borrow one of mine. Despite the kidlets there, you'll swim in it."

She laughed. "Politely put."

"What?"

"Saving my feelings over being so huge by telling me your jacket would be too big."

He grinned. "I'm the soul of discretion. I do have some experience with pregnant women and their touchy moods."

"What kind of experience?"

"Three of my best friends, Wyatt, Ethan and Stony, have had pregnant wives. I've commiserated a lot."

"Mm, and you learned a lesson in tact?"

"I learn well."

She smiled and snuggled into his side. The air had a definite bite to it, and the weatherman was predicting snow. Although it was only early November, storefronts were already festive with holiday decorations.

"Think we'll have snow for Christmas?"

"We usually do."

"I love this season. Everything's so happy and bright. It'll be the babies' first Christmas."

"Probably be a bit young to fully appreciate it."

"Don't be a killjoy. They'll be mesmerized by the lights. Wait and see."

He looked down at her for a long moment, his dark eyes holding her as softly as a caress.

"You'll be a great mother, Emily."

Her heart did a wild leap.

He squeezed her shoulder, hugged her closer. "Have you decided if you'll be Auntie or Mommy?"

Emily's heart stung. This was an issue she was still unsure about. She'd never dreamed she'd be put in a position to have to make that choice. Her emotions were all over the place, and frankly, when she allowed herself to be totally honest, she had to admit that she was still indulging in quite a bit of denial, as though she'd wake up in the morning and it would all be a bad dream. As though Debbie and Jimmy would be here fussing over her, holding hands, anticipating, pinching themselves over their coveted, long-awaited blessings.

"There's time to decide," she said softly. "I want the kids to know about Debbie and Jimmy, to realize they were conceived as a result of their parents' deep love. I don't want to take away from that in any way."

He stopped next to the truck, pulled her around to face him. For the longest moment he simply looked down at her. Then he oh-so-gently pressed his lips to her forehead, her eyelids and at last to her lips.

She wanted to cling, but the contact was over before she could think twice or even figure out what she'd said or done to bring on that incredibly tender look, that incredibly tender touch.

"What was that for?"

"For you. Just you. I bet my brother and your sister are looking down, thanking God they entrusted their children to such an extraordinary woman."

Tears swam in her eyes and she blinked them back. She wasn't so extraordinary.

But she reveled in the compliment.

And felt way too comfortable, too right, in Cheyenne Bodine's arms.

Chapter Six

Cheyenne had the dresser in place and the crib set up, and was testing the spring action of the side. The room was transformed into a sea of white with vibrant red accents. Appliqués of happy bears and lambs frolicked on the shiny white wood, the theme was repeated on the bumper pads and sheets.

They'd ended up only buying one crib, each of them citing financial thriftiness for the decision, each of them knowing that wasn't the case at all. By the time the babies grew enough to need their own space, it would be time for Emily to leave.

"Look at how tiny these are." Emily held up a little shirt that was hardly bigger than her hand. "Maybe we should have gotten a larger size. This doesn't look like it'd fit a grasshopper."

Cheyenne glanced over at her and smiled. "They'll be fine."

"Well, I guess you'd know better than me. You've been around more babies." She folded the T-shirts and put them in the drawer along with the fluffy blankets, sleepers and tiny socks. "I've never even held one."

"A baby? You're kidding!"

"Nope." She lightly ran her hands over the soft fabric of a drawstring gown. Besides the neutral colors of yellow and green, she'd also bought pink outfits. If she had boys, they could just alternate wearing the girl color. She'd start them young learning to be secure in their masculinity.

Listen to me, she thought with a silent chuckle. *Already worrying over their self-esteem.*

It was all starting to feel real. For the first time she allowed herself to picture babies in the crib, sweet little angels swaddled in blankets. *Her* babies.

Yes, they were her babies now.

Surrounding herself with the trappings seemed to make something inside her go click.

She hadn't chosen this path, but she would do her best. For Debbie. And for Jimmy. And for Cheyenne and the children.

Cheyenne's words came back to her. *Will you be Auntie or Mommy?*

The idea of the babies calling her Mommy made her heart soften and flutter. Still, she felt a real fear that she might fail. She didn't know why. She was a person who faced responsibility head-on. But what if that wasn't enough?

She placed a hand on her stomach, where the babies were inactive for once. Come to think of it, they'd been inactive most of the day. She'd probably worn them out with all the walking. She would love these children. She already loved them....

Emily's eyes widened and she sucked in a breath.

"What's wrong?" Cheyenne was at her side in an instant. Did the man have radar? The last she'd checked, he'd been engrossed in the spring mechanism of the crib.

"I'm not sure. I just had a sharp pain, and...oh, my God, my water just broke!"

He stared at her as though she'd told him Santa's reindeers were sharing the barn with his mustangs.

"Are you sure?"

"Of course I'm sure! I'm the one standing here with a mess all over my shoes!"

"Sit down. On second thought..." He scooped her up in his arms.

"Cheyenne! For heaven's—"

"Hush. I'm not letting you out of my sight." He strode through the house and deposited her on the couch. "Stay put. I'll call Chance."

She knew she should have made more of an effort to meet with the doctor Chance had recommended. "I'm not having these babies at home."

"Just calm down."

"Oh, that's right. You try to be calm with water running down your legs and two babies who've decided to come out. It wasn't supposed to be—oooh."

Cheyenne dropped the phone he'd just picked up. "What?"

Tears stung her eyes. She was going to be a sissy about this. She was sure of it. "I think I'm in labor," she panted.

"What should I do?"

"How the hell should I know? You're the one with the baby-delivering experience!"

"I'm not delivering these babies!" His jaw was tight, his voice a soft growl, his hands gentle as he squatted in front of her, rubbed her arms, her thighs, watched her as she panted through the short pain.

Figures he'd be the calm, quiet one when she was the screaming meemie. Then again, *she* was the one feeling as if her insides were ripping apart.

"Is it over?"

"I think so." She was trembling, her nails digging half-moons in his forearms. "I didn't mean to yell at you. I'm scared to death."

"Yeah, me, too. Hang on and let me call Chance."

He got up and retrieved the phone, then brought it to the couch and stood right over her as he punched in numbers on the portable.

"Chance? Cheyenne. Emily's in labor." A pause. "Two pains so far. Her water broke." He listened another minute. "Okay. We'll meet you there. On second thought, I've got to pass through town on the way to the hospital. Fall in behind my truck. If things get hairy on the road, I want backup." He nodded, listened some more, then hung up.

"Let's go."

"Shouldn't I pack a bag or something?"

"Do you want to hang around here any longer than necessary?"

She shook her head.

"Thought not." He helped her to her feet, threaded

her arms through the sleeves of her coat and walked her outside. ''We'll take the Bronco.''

She grinned. For all his quiet tone, he was a mass of terrified male. It was endearing.

Despite his nerves, though, she knew she was in capable hands. ''We get the whole treatment, huh? Lights and siren and all?''

''If need be.''

''Saves having to explain if we get stopped for speeding.''

''Only *you* get stopped for speeding, trouble.''

EMILY WANTED to change her mind. She didn't want to do this, didn't want to go through any more. She wanted to go home.

She'd been wrenched in pain for six hours, was so tired she just wanted to curl up somewhere and sleep for a year.

Which wasn't an option. Whoever said hospitals were supposed to be quiet out of respect for the sick? She was hooked up to monitors that beeped and carried on and drove both her and Cheyenne nuts.

Her room resembled Grand Central Station, with everyone coming in and out. Chance was there for moral support and appeared to be the only calm one in the bunch.

Dr. Freeman had come in to check on her twice and pronounced that she was progressing nicely, though she did discuss the possibility of a cesarean delivery.

At this point Emily didn't care how the babies were delivered. She just wanted them out.

And though she'd refused them so far, drugs were starting to sound like a good option.

"Why does the heart rate keep going down?" Cheyenne asked, watching the monitor at her bedside as the numbers ran up and down.

"It's just another contraction," Chance told him calmly, resting his fingers on Emily's wrist, checking her pulse. "You're doing fine, Emily. Take a deep breath. Breathe through it."

"*Just* another?" Emily said between pants. "Do *you* want to get in this bed? And I am *not* doing fine!" The pain was like a clawing, snarling beast, clamping its vicious jaws over her abdomen. Multiply the pain of cramps by about a zillion and it still wouldn't even come close to what she was experiencing.

With the arm that wasn't attached to the IV, she grabbed for Cheyenne's hand, squeezing so hard he winced. *Good,* she thought. *I hope it hurts like hell.*

"I need some drugs. Cheyenne, tell him to get me something... Oh, damn it."

"Almost there, sweetheart," Cheyenne coached.

"Shut up." She breathed and panted and forgot which breath sequence she was supposed to be doing. Like anybody knew when she was almost there, she thought. The pains were coming closer together, and it was hard to tell when one stopped and the next began.

Why the hell had she ever thought she could be strong about this, get through this without pain-numbing medication?

Never mind that Chance's explanation of the epidural had scared the stuffing right out of her. More than pain, Emily hated needles!

The pressure was increasing and her emotions were escalating toward outright terror. She didn't want these babies popping out when no one was looking.

She liked to be in control, liked to know in advance exactly how things were laid out, how they would work. When facing anything new and untried, she liked to make a trial run, to work out any glitches in the beginning, to make sure she knew exactly where she was going so there would be no surprises.

Childbirth didn't allow for trial runs. And the fear of the unknown was taunting her like a salivating ghoul with an echoing sinister laugh.

"Isn't it time yet?"

"Should we page the doctor?" Cheyenne asked.

"Just…just *look*, damn it," Emily said to Chance. "I don't even care anymore." Childbirth turned modesty to dust.

Donna, the labor nurse, stepped up to the end of the bed. "I'll check. Do you want the men to leave the room?"

Emily's fingers tightened even more around Cheyenne's. She'd done nothing but bark at him for the past hour, but he was her lifeline. She didn't want him budging from her side. "No. I'm sorry I'm being such a baby."

Donna patted her knee and draped the sheet so that her modesty was somewhat preserved and donned a pair of gloves. "I suspect you're in the transition stage, and moms tend to get a little testy at this point."

She did a quick examination, then smiled. "Just as I thought. Dilated about nine centimeters and eighty-percent effaced."

"What does that mean?"

"That means I'll page Dr. Freeman now," Chance said.

She wanted these babies out, but now her fear had shot right off the charts. *Almost time.*

"Can't you do it?" she asked Chance.

"I thought you wanted someone else."

"I changed my mind."

He nodded. "I have privileges here. If that's what you want, I can deliver the babies."

"Yes. That's what I want— Oh!"

"Again?" Cheyenne asked, and automatically moved into her line of vision, trying to give her comfort, a focal point. His composure was shot to hell. He'd seen childbirth, but it hadn't been this personal. It hadn't seemed this painful. It hadn't been Emily.

He wanted to take her pain, bear it for her.

All he could do was hold her hand and stroke her face and ache right along with her.

He didn't dare tell her he could practically feel each one of her contractions. He had an idea she'd hit him.

And judging by the death grip she had on his hand, she could probably lay him out cold in a single blow.

The nurse was still at the end of the bed. "We're there," she announced.

"Where?" Emily shrieked. "What do you mean we're there?"

"I can see hair."

"Don't say that!" Emily's voice a near hysterical shout.

Cheyenne's heart was pounding and he was light-headed. My God, he was going to embarrass himself before this was all over. He was sure of it.

Chance reached for Emily's free hand. "Don't push now."

"Easy for you to say." Her voice trembled. "It feels like something's happening."

"I know. It won't be long. I'll go scrub in and see you in the delivery room."

"You can't leave! Donna said there's hair!"

Cheyenne wanted to add his own objections. Emily was on the verge of tears again, and he was right there on the edge with her. But she needed his strength now, not his worries.

"It's just a quick trip down the hall, Em. A couple of minutes. Chance will hurry."

"Run," Emily suggested.

Chance grinned. "I'm running. You coming, Cheyenne?"

"I don't—"

"He's coming!" Emily insisted.

And Cheyenne found himself dragged along, whether he wanted to be or not. He was barely able to pull his hand out of Emily's grasp as they loaded her onto a gurney.

The biggest part of him wanted to experience every facet of this incredible miracle. The small cowardly part, the *male* part, wanted to pace—at a safe distance in the fathers' waiting room.

Fathers' waiting room.

God, he wished Jimmy were here.

He followed Chance to wash his hands and get out-fitted in scrubs, all the while worried about Emily, not liking the separation.

Despite Chance's calm demeanor, the doctor moved quickly. That heightened Cheyenne's anxiety. "She'll be okay, won't she?"

"I don't anticipate any problems. She's had a normal pregnancy, but multiple births always increase the risk. It's best to be prepared for anything, so if something does come up and I ask you to leave, do it quickly."

Cheyenne stopped and looked his friend in the eye. "Don't put either of us in that position."

It was difficult to appear tough wearing a paper cap over his hair, but he managed to convey it nonetheless. He could tell by the respect he saw in the doctor's eyes.

Still, there was hesitation. "Cheyenne—"

"I mean it, Chance. I'm all she's got and there's no way in hell I'll abandon her if things get rough. Once I walk through that door, I'm staying. Got it?"

"I could fix it so you don't walk through that door in the first place."

They stared at each other like enemies facing off in battle. "Do you really want to try that?"

Chance let out a breath and shook his head. "It's going to go fine. You'll see. But I swear, if you faint, I'm telling the whole town."

"I'll take out the ad myself."

The minute he stepped into the delivery room, Emily reached for him. The relief in her eyes at the sight of him made his heart squeeze.

Her hair was mashed to her head, curling wildly at her damp temples, sticking up at odd places. Her skin was pale, her eyelids swollen, her fingernails ragged where the acrylics had been removed.

She'd never looked more beautiful.

"How you doing, trouble?"

"I need to push. Tell him, I need to push," she said as though Chance wasn't standing right there at her bedside with perfectly fine hearing.

"Just a couple more minutes," Chance said to Emily. "Right now, we're going to put a little something in the IV to relax you."

"It won't affect the babies, will it?"

"No. Try not to touch the drape. We want to keep it sterile."

"Maybe you should just knock me out. I'm whipped. I don't think—" She sucked in a breath and grabbed for her stomach.

Cheyenne took her hands in his, glanced at Chance. He felt so helpless. And he felt light-headed again, damn it. "What should I do?"

"Think long and hard before you speak in the next few minutes."

Astonishingly Emily laughed, even though she was obviously in the throes of a contraction. "I'm sorry. I don't know why I feel like acting so ugly."

"You're entitled. Breathe, baby. Hold on to me."

"I'm trying. Ouch! What was that?"

"Just general anesthetic."

"I told you I hate needles!"

"Shh," Cheyenne consoled. "You're tough." Still, he glared at Chance.

"All done," Chance said, grinning. "Take a breath now. Cheyenne, raise her up and support her back. Push with this contraction, Emily. To the count of ten. Let's get these babies introduced to the world."

Through a whole lot of swearing, a whole lot of sweating, Cheyenne held her, pushed with her, breathed with her, ached with her. Tears leaked out of her eyes and he wanted to cry right along with her.

He was so focused on Emily, wishing like hell he didn't feel so helpless, it was a minute before he realized a baby was crying.

"What is it?" Emily asked. "Are they both here?"

"A little boy. Fine one, too." Chance held the squalling infant up, then laid him on Emily's stomach.

"Can I touch him?" she asked.

"Yes."

With her hand still attached to the IV, she stroked the infant's slick dark hair. Cheyenne's hand covered hers, nearly spanning the baby's whole body.

"He's so small." She was laughing and crying and trembling. Then another vicious pain wrenched her belly.

"He's a keeper," Chance said. "Round two. Almost over, Emily. You're doing great."

The nurse picked up the baby and Cheyenne raised Emily into position.

Emily thought her strength was all used up, but with

the excitement of seeing the little baby, she got a burst of energy. Or she thought so, until she tried to push and couldn't hold the count.

"Wait!"

"Come on, sweetheart. Don't give up on me now."

"I can't do it."

"Yes, you can. I'm right here."

She felt Cheyenne's lips at her temple, his breath warm against her, his arms around her. She took another breath and bore down. She was beyond pain, beyond thinking. Time stood still and she felt like a spectator, floating above the scene, watching as the woman turned red in the face and the man held her gently.

And at last a second lusty cry joined the first.

"One of each," Chance said. "A little girl this time. Two minutes younger than her brother."

She was shaking uncontrollably, her legs, her hands. And was so cold.

"Is she all right?"

"She's perfect," Cheyenne said, kissing her cheeks, her eyelids, her lips. "I'm so proud of you."

A nurse was wiping the babies off, weighing and measuring them. "Six pounds, four ounces for the girl, six pounds even for the boy."

"Oh, she'll hate that," Emily said, through a watery laugh, her teeth chattering. "I don't think we'll tell her she weighed more than her brother."

The pediatric nurse took one of the tightly wrapped infants and put it in Emily's arms, then handed the other to Cheyenne.

The warm little bundle was soft and peaceful, with round cheeks and a red face that looked like it had gotten a sunburn and was peeling.

Emily hadn't exaggerated when she'd said she'd never held an infant before. And my gosh, this one had come from her body!

"Which do I have? The boy or girl?"

"The girl. Cheyenne's holding the boy."

She glanced at him, and the utterly profound look of awe and reverence on his face brought tears to her eyes.

He met her gaze. "You're amazing."

She didn't feel very amazing. She felt worn to a frazzle. "Debbie and Jimmy would be so proud," she whispered.

She saw his eyes swim with tears that never fell.

"Yes, they would." He placed the second baby in her free arm so she could cuddle them both and pressed a kiss to each tiny head and then to Emily's forehead.

She gazed at both babies. "Do you know what Jimmy's middle name was?"

"Hunter. James Hunter."

"Do you think…they never decided on names because we didn't know the sex of the babies. What do you think about naming them after Debbie and Jimmy, using their middle names? Hunter James, and Alicia Debra?"

"Hunter and Alicia Bodine." His Adam's apple bobbed. "I think my brother and your sister would approve."

Chance cleared his throat. "Okay, you two, there's still some work to do yet."

With her focus solely on her new family, she'd nearly forgotten about the doctor.

The nurses took the babies and Emily grabbed for Cheyenne's hand.

"I have a feeling this next part is going to involve needles," she said to Chance.

"You won't feel a thing—maybe a little tug, but that's it. You did a fine job, Emily. Not even a hitch. Guess you've got one of those bodies made for having babies."

That was news to Emily. But just as her body had adapted perfectly to the embryo transplant, it had seemed in fine working order for delivery.

She could have done with a little less pain, though.

EMILY STAYED in the hospital for three days. Although a lot of mothers went home right away, Emily had claimed she was a wimp and so was happy to stay exactly where she was, thank you very much.

Cheyenne was actually glad that she and the babies were getting around-the-clock professional care. Because when they came home, they would be in his care.

He hoped he was up to the task. Man alive, those little tykes were small.

After taking care of the release papers, he made his way to Emily's room. She wasn't in the bed.

He found her in the tiny bathroom, sitting on the closed lid of the commode.

Crying.

In one step he was at her side. "What is it? Are you in pain? Did you hurt yourself?"

She shook her head. "I can't get into my pants," she whispered between sniffs.

He was lost.

"I even brought my fat jeans!"

Fat jeans? "Can't you just wear those stretchy things you wore to the hospital?" It was a reasonable-enough suggestion.

Or so he thought.

She glared at him, the spark in her green eyes equivalent to a punch. *Uh-oh.*

"They're *maternity* pants! I'm not *pregnant* anymore."

And to his consternation, she burst into renewed sobs.

Cheyenne was like a drowning man down for the count.

"Um, do you want me to call the nurse?"

"If you say one more stupid thing, I'm going to hit you!"

Well, hell. He knelt in front of her, tipped up her chin.

"Do you know how incredible you are?"

She rolled her eyes.

He cupped her cheeks, pressed a lingering kiss to her forehead.

"I'm a mess."

"A beautiful mess."

She gave a watery laugh. "And I'm acting like a baby."

"Hell, trouble, you're entitled. I was in that delivery room with you, too. It was bad enough as a bystander. I couldn't have done what you did."

She bit her lips, sniffed again. "Well, if you want to know the truth, I impressed the daylights out of myself."

He grinned. "Atta girl. At the risk of bodily injury, do you want me to bring in your other clothes?"

"I guess."

"You could just wear your gown and robe home if you want."

"Please. My dignity's smarting enough as it is."

He rose to do her bidding.

"Did you bring outfits for the kids?" she asked.

"Already dropped them off in the nursery. They're taking pictures."

"That's nice. Cheyenne?"

He stopped and looked back.

"Thanks for putting up with me."

"Anytime, trouble." He didn't tell her how easy she was to "put up with."

He wanted to do it for a lifetime. And knew it was only for a while.

EMILY CURSED her independent streak, called herself every kind of idiot for insisting she'd be fine while Cheyenne handled some emergency sheriff business. He'd hated to leave her on her first full day at home, offered to get one of the neighbors over to sit with her, but she'd felt cocky.

He'd only expected to be gone a couple of hours. No sense imposing on the neighbors.

The babies had been asleep.

Well, they were wide awake now, and all hell had broken loose.

Even the dog was thoroughly disgusted with the chaos and racket. He was curled up on a pillow by the fireplace, obviously trying to make himself invisible lest he be pressed into service. Emily didn't blame him. She felt like hiding, too. How had this happened?

Well, she knew now it had happened. She'd opened her mouth and agreed to be a human incubator for her sister's babies.

"Oh, Debbie," she whispered, "you can't imagine how much I wish you were here." The tears that were never far from the surface ached in her throat, swam in her eyes.

She'd been like an ostrich, sticking her head in the sand, trying to ignore what was to come. In some ridiculous corner of her mind, the part that had been in near-complete denial, she'd figured if she didn't think about it, it might all go away.

Or maybe she'd thought that when the babies arrived, she'd simply handle it, catch on, and if that were the case, there was no sense worrying herself half to death.

Well, she should have worried *much* sooner!

She didn't know what she'd expected. She'd definitely been in denial, she realized now, like playing dolls as a child. Pretend.

It hadn't totally registered that this was reality.

Now reality hit her full force with squalling babies, diaper changes every two minutes, sheer terror over every hiccup and choking sound.

This wasn't playing house with a pretend mommy and daddy and baby.

She couldn't put away the dolls.

Oh, she'd had it all planned out so nicely. While Cheyenne was gone, she'd make a few phone calls, pump a couple of bottles of breast milk, watch the two little cherubs sleep and marvel at how precious they were.

Nothing was going as planned.

The baby nursing at her left breast wasn't cooperating, and every time she tried to make an adjustment, the other baby—who was propped on a pillow in her lap—got jostled and lost its hold on the nipple of the bottle she'd popped in its mouth.

Both were squalling again and she had no idea which baby was which. They'd both messed up their clothes, and during the last horrendously scary clothing change, she'd forgotten which color she'd dressed which kid in.

Short of undressing them and looking at their identifying equipment, she hadn't a clue who was nursing and who was drinking breast milk from the bottle.

So much for organization.

"Okay, okay," she soothed, perilously close to tears herself. "Let's try something different."

With a lot of fussing and very little finesse, she switched the babies' positions, putting the one in her lap to her right breast and managing to get the other one settled with the bottle.

She gave a fleeting thought to the sanitary issue of their sharing the same bottle without her sterilizing the nipple, and decided it was simply too bad.

She felt like a dairy cow. Her life suddenly revolved around feeding. If the babies weren't nursing, she was pumping the stuff into the bottles.

It had all seemed much more civilized in the hospital.

Where had she gone wrong?

And what was the matter with her technique? Now neither of the kids was cooperating.

She gave up, feeling like a total failure. She could organize a whole boardroom full of disagreeable advertising executives but couldn't handle two tiny babies.

She was so tired, she wanted to lie down and die.

The front door opened and a blast of cold air rushed in.

Emily quickly adjusted her shirt and pulled a blanket over the babies.

Now they were both screaming beneath a tent.

She took one look at Cheyenne and burst into tears.

"Here now," he said softly. He removed his gloves and hat, then lifted the babies, who were now lying side by side in her lap, screaming their little lungs out, into his arms.

The fact that he lifted them so easily and capably made her cry even harder.

She buried her face in her hands, then jolted a few minutes later when she felt Cheyenne's fingers brush the top of her head.

She looked up, saw him standing over her with concern written all over his handsome face. "Where are the babies?"

"I put them in the crib."

"But they're still crying!" *Duh.*

"So are you."

Double duh. She felt like an idiot. "We have to take care of them."

"We have to take care of you first. They'll be fine for a few minutes. It won't hurt them to cry."

He picked her up and carried her down the hall and into the bathroom. She didn't have enough energy to object.

He set her down on the closed lid of the toilet and said, "Stay put."

"I can't—"

"Let me call the shots, trouble."

"Yeah, that's me. Plenty of trouble."

He bent down and kissed her forehead, then left the room.

Minutes later the babies quieted.

The lack of sound was like a taunt, a screaming billboard that advertised to the world that Emily Vincent Bodine didn't have a clue how to handle two little babies.

Emily wept again.

Chapter Seven

"What is it?" Cheyenne asked when he came back into the bathroom.

"They're not crying anymore. Why wouldn't they stop doing that for me?" She was a mess. Her hair was sticking out, her orange flannel shirt was stained and didn't match the green stretch pants. Neither did her wool socks, she realized. One was black and the other navy blue. How had this happened? Probably when she'd had to change her clothes along with the babies'.

She was a walking fashion disaster.

And she was *still* wearing the damned maternity pants!

She put her hands over her face as though that would somehow make her invisible.

When she heard the bathwater running, she peeked through her fingers, then lowered her hands.

"I don't have time for this."

"Yes. You'll take time."

"I think I should warn you that if you keep bossing

me around like this, I'll still be crying a week from now.''

He shuddered. "Please don't."

She wished she could laugh. "I'm stronger than this. I don't cry. I'm just...I'm so sorry." In more ways than one.

"You've been strong for everybody—for so long. Please let me take care of you."

Oh, no. When he spoke to her in that deep, soft, incredibly compassionate voice, she was a goner. She held her breath. Swallowed several times. It didn't help. The emotions were more than she could handle. Fresh tears slid down her cheeks.

"Oh, baby. Don't." He scooped her up, traded places and sat with her in his lap.

"I'm sorry. I've never acted this way in my life."

"I shouldn't have left you alone so soon."

She sniffed and laid her head against his shoulder. He smelled like fresh air and masculinity. "I carried those babies in my womb for nine months. You'd think I'd be better at this. That I'd know what to do."

"You'll catch your stride."

"When? When they're in college?"

He chuckled and started to help her undress.

"Wait!"

His hands paused over the buttons. "Can you manage on your own?"

"I managed while you were gone. Maybe you didn't notice, but I don't think I looked quite this bad when you left."

"You look just fine. And I'm sorry I had to leave

you. I've taken vacation time, so it won't happen again.''

"I'm already messing up your life.''

"You're not messing up my life." He stood and deposited her on her feet, then reached for a brush on the countertop and rummaged in the drawer for a hair band. Shutting off the bathwater, he gently gathered her hair in his hands.

"What are you doing?" Chills raced up and down her spine.

"Did you want to get your hair wet?"

"No. It takes forever to dry, but—"

"Then I'm going to put it up for you. Don't expect miracles, but at least this'll keep it off your shoulders.''

She closed her eyes as he ran a brush through her thick, frizzy hair, lifting it, corralling it in a soft fabric band.

Steam from the water fogged the mirror, filled the air with moist heat and a sense of expectancy she couldn't name. The sensual, saunalike atmosphere, coupled with Cheyenne's gentle ministrations, moved something inside her.

She moaned, felt him go still behind her.

Embarrassment flooded her. What in the world? Her nose was red, her eyes were swollen, not a stitch of her clothing matched, and here she'd been flirting with sensual thoughts, assigning sensual thoughts to him, too.

"Um, I think I can handle it from here.''

She didn't look at him. Couldn't look at him.

Because she wanted in the worse way to turn in his arms, to press up against him, to kiss him, to feel his body respond to hers...

Good grief.

"I'll be right outside the door. Give a yell if you need anything."

She nodded. She needed something all right. Like less-wild hormones.

Who ever heard of sexual desire, *acute* sexual desire, waylaying a woman this soon after childbirth?

THE BABIES WERE ASLEEP at last and Emily was curled on the couch in Cheyenne's arms. She probably shouldn't be cuddling this way. It felt too right. Too much like a truly married couple.

But she couldn't make herself move.

"Do you think they sent us home with the wrong babies?"

She felt his chest shake as he let out a soft burst of laughter. "I think they've got a pretty good system in place to keep that from happening."

"Well, the ones in the hospital were certainly better behaved than these two."

He chuckled again. "We'll all find our step soon enough."

And then she'd be gone. She would have accomplished her goal. To get the hang of taking care of the babies.

The thought made her sad.

On the other hand, her behavior today didn't exactly

make her a good contender for the mother-of-the-year award.

"I'm sorry I fell apart today."

"Chance said this sort of thing is normal."

"You called him?"

"Yeah. I was worried."

She sighed. "Couldn't keep the embarrassment just between us, hmm?"

He stroked her arm. "Nothing to be embarrassed about."

"You're too kind. What did Chance say?"

"He'll be out tomorrow to check on you and the kids."

She nodded. "I'll feel better, I'm sure. It's ridiculous, really. I'm not normally inept. I've blazed my way nearly to the top of my field, and a woman doesn't accomplish that feat without intelligence, drive and a whole lot of strength. Yet those two little babies knocked me right on my butt."

"I wasn't far behind you."

She shifted against him, watched the flames in the fireplace, listened to the crackle as the log split and a shower of sparks were sucked up the flue. Outside, snowflakes swirled, gathering on the windowsill, only to be blown away by the wind.

She shivered and burrowed closer, telling herself she'd pull back in a minute.

"You know what worries me?"

"What?" His voice was quiet, his fingers gentle as they stroked her arm.

"That I won't have enough time or arms or love to go around."

He frowned. "You won't?"

"With two of them, it's hard, you know? I just want to hold the babies, stare into their sweet faces. But how do you do that when they both need attention? What if one of them ends up being slighted?"

"That's what you have me for. Between the two of us, we can manage."

"Do you think they feel it—that I'm not really their mother?"

"Emily, you are their mother. In every sense of the word. You're not giving yourself enough credit."

"It just feels... I can't explain it. I look at those babies and I feel so full of love. But I feel so scared still. Debbie was the maternal one. She was the quintessential earth mother, made her own bread, sewed curtains, ate health food. She read cookbooks and parenting magazines, and when she wasn't working at the day care center, she baby-sat all the neighbors' kids." Emily's throat ached, but she told herself she wasn't going to cry any more today. "I miss her," she whispered.

"I know."

"Why do bad things happen to such good people?"

He shook his head. Silence engulfed them.

"I don't bake bread or sew, and my idea of healthy eating is a salad at a fast-food joint. I went to the day care center a couple of times, and I thought the kids were cute, but I never had the urge to ask if I could hold any of the babies."

"Neither have I."

"You're a guy."

His sensual mouth kicked up at the corners. "Glad you noticed."

She laughed. "See what I mean? I'm so frazzled I was starting to look at you like you were a piece of furniture." Which was as far from the truth as possible.

"Low blow. Maybe we should do something about that."

"Like what?" She really wasn't in top form. Otherwise she'd never have asked such an inane question, would have understood right off the bat what he was talking about. She didn't date much, but she knew the flirting game, knew when a man was looking at her with sex on his mind.

And Cheyenne was definitely looking at her with sex on his mind.

It was absolutely amazing. After the way she'd acted today, so totally inept, the way she looked. In her opinion, there wasn't a chance in creation that a man would find anything remotely sexy about her.

But Cheyenne obviously did.

With his finger, he tipped up her chin. His eyes were dark and serious. She could see the faint shadow of stubble on his face.

She held her breath, certain this wasn't a good idea, helpless to move, feeling like prey caught in the hypnotic gaze of the hunter.

His head lowered.

"We shouldn't be—"

"I know," he said, and brushed her lips with his.

Fire, she thought. She was on fire. She shifted against him, turned into him, cupped her hand around the back of his neck and held him closer, harder, encouraging him to take the kiss further, deeper.

He made her feel like a woman. And she desperately needed that right now. After the day she'd had, she needed this. Just this.

She felt his control and wished he'd unleash it. She tried to convey that, moaned into his mouth, twisted closer, nearly climbing onto his lap.

He tucked her against him, poured himself into the kiss. His tongue was warm and clever, tasted of coffee and masculinity. Tasted of seduction and protection.

And she wanted more. So much more.

A faint cry penetrated her consciousness.

Cheyenne broke the kiss, his breath coming as fast as hers.

"Whoa, that went a little further than I'd intended."

Not nearly far enough, Emily thought.

And then reality settled around her. What in the world had she been thinking? She'd practically begged for that kiss. As though she was needy.

Good grief. Hadn't she displayed enough of that neediness today?

Both babies were crying now. Blue was on his feet, glancing toward the hall, then back at Cheyenne and Emily as though they were falling down on the job. It was time she took care of business, showed a little strength, some competence.

But she still only had one set of arms.

And two babies to hold.

She saw Cheyenne's gaze settle on her chest and she looked down. To her utter mortification, she realized the front of her sweatshirt was drenched—and so was his shirt.

Her face flamed. *Well, this is sexy as all get-out,* she thought grimly.

She eased off the couch, winced a little as her stitches tugged. Because she'd compartmentalized the pregnancy as a service, distanced herself from it, she was continually amazed that her body did all these perfectly normal things—like produce milk.

Cheyenne stood with her, steadied her. "Boy or girl?"

"What?" She was still trying to figure out how to gracefully apologize for leaking all over the front of him.

"You want Alicia or Hunter?"

"Oh." She moved toward the nursery. "We might have to unwrap them to tell which is which. I ran out of color-coordinated clothes and lost track."

"Color-coordinated"

"Yes. I was trying to dress Hunter in blue and Alicia in pink so I could tell them apart."

"Alicia's face is rounder. And her lips are more bowed."

She stopped in the middle of the hall and he nearly ran into her. "You can tell them apart?"

"Yes."

She stared up at him for a full five seconds. Then

she whirled around and marched into the nursery, examining both squalling babies.

And there it was. Alicia's cheeks were definitely chubbier.

Oh, this was just awful.

Why hadn't she seen this? Cheyenne was a man. *He* was more maternal than she was.

WHEN THEY GOT the babies fed and back to sleep, Emily followed Cheyenne down the hall.

''Night,'' he said, knowing they'd probably be up in a couple hours again.

''Night.'' He could tell she was dead on her feet.

And so was he. They'd both almost nodded off in the rocking chairs.

He lay down on the bed and was astonished when Emily followed him right into the room, crawled across the mattress and fell into a dead sleep against him.

For a minute he didn't move a muscle. He didn't think she'd realized she'd gotten into his bed, instead of her own.

Should he point it out? Be a good guy and put her in her own bed?

She snuggled next to him. Nah, he decided, and shifted her so that his arm was around her. Her hair smelled of vanilla and baby powder. An erotic combination.

The feel of her soft breasts pillowed on his chest was going to keep him awake. He couldn't remember ever being this tired in his life. He had an idea he hadn't yet learned the true meaning of the word.

Because with Emily's body snuggled next to his, he had little chance of sleeping.

WEAK SUNSHINE filtered through the curtains. Emily snuggled closer to the warmth against her side. Then her eyes popped open.

Cheyenne was staring down at her.

She gazed at him for several seconds, memories shuffling in her mind like a deck of cards. A few were missing.

She eased away. "How did this happen?"

"You followed me to bed. I didn't have the heart to wake you and point out the error."

"Sorry."

"Mmm. I don't mind sharing my bed with a beautiful woman."

"Beautiful, hah! Lack of sleep has fried your brain." There was no sense giving in to embarrassment. This was mild compared to what she'd done already.

She paused, listened, then leaped out of the bed.

"What's the matter?"

"The babies."

"I don't hear them."

"Exactly! There must be something wrong!" She raced out of the room.

Cheyenne followed. Standing by the side of the crib, she looked over her shoulder at him.

"They're still asleep," she whispered.

"Which is what you should be doing."

"What about you?"

"I need to see about the horses."

Emily had forgotten he had animals counting on him, too. Poor guy. He was responsible for the safety of the town, a stable of horses and her and the babies. All she had right now were the kids.

"I've dumped a lot of responsibility on you, haven't I?"

"My shoulders are wide."

And very nice, she thought. "Do you have time for breakfast? I could make you something."

A dimple creased his cheek. "As in cooking?"

She glared. "If I put my mind to it, I can cook."

His brow climbed.

"I never said I *couldn't* cook. Just that I didn't do it often. Besides, we still have those yummy scones that Eden made. A quick zap in the microwave and a healthy squirt of butter, and we'll be set for the day."

"I'll settle for coffee right now. Hopefully I can get the horses fed before the little ones wake up."

AS IT TURNED OUT, he didn't have to hurry, because the neighbors showed up, bearing food and willing arms and an easy capability that put Emily's own abilities to shame.

Hannah Malone came first.

"Where are the children?" Emily asked, juggling Hunter in her arms as she let the other woman in.

"I dropped them off with Dora Callahan." She put a casserole dish in the refrigerator and scooped Alicia out of the infant seat where the baby was beginning to work herself into a fine fuss. "Dora's got a new litter of kittens she's photographing, and my son, Ian, can't resist baby animals. Shh, darling," she cooed to the baby who immediately hushed and blinked owllike eyes.

"Why is she taking pictures of baby animals?"

"She's a freelance photographer—an artist, really. She does those cute greeting cards and posters. Puts flower wreaths on Ethan's foals and steals the cowboys' hats for props." Hannah laughed. "Dora's got a way with babies and animals and people, but don't count on her to whip your kitchen into shape."

As though they'd choreographed it in advance, Emily handed Hannah a bottle for Alicia, then sat down to nurse Hunter.

"I don't know if anyone could whip this kitchen into shape. The babies are up for two minutes and it looks like a bomb exploded. I don't have enough hands—or arms."

"I understand. It's difficult enough with one." She nuzzled Alicia's cheek and eased a bottle into her cupid's-bow mouth. "The babies are precious."

"Thank you." Emily winced and tried to get Hunter to nurse. "I'm not very good at this."

"It'll get easier with each day."

Emily laughed. "One hopes, anyway. Cheyenne's been a godsend."

"He's a good man. A little hard to get to know. I can't tell you how much we admire the two of you for what you're doing."

Emily's head jerked up.

"Uh-oh. I see you're not quite used to the information grapevine. I hope I haven't made you uncomfortable."

Emily thought about that for a minute. True, she wasn't used to being the topic of conversation, but it didn't really bother her that people knew the circumstances of Alicia and Hunter's birth.

"No. You haven't made me uncomfortable. There are people in this town who remember my sister and Cheyenne's brother. And I want my children to know who their parents were. I don't want them forgotten." She didn't realize she'd so easily said *my* children.

"You lived here before?"

"When I was a girl."

"Then you've known Cheyenne for a while."

"Not really." *In my secret dreams—forever.* Talking about Cheyenne put her emotions in a turmoil. She didn't want to think about what he stirred up in her right now. For goodness' sake, she'd slept with him. Granted, it was only sleeping, but still...

"So, how did you meet Wyatt?"

Hannah didn't even blink at the subject change. "I was his mail-order bride."

"Oh." That sounded fairly old-fashioned, but Emily told herself it was none of her business.

"I can see your curiosity. I was in California, a single mother of a four-year-old and pregnant with Meredith. I'd dreamed of life on a ranch—which seems odd, given that I was scared to death of animals, the dogs included. Anyway, before I'd allowed myself time to think it through, I'd answered an ad that Wyatt knew nothing about.''

"He didn't advertise for a bride?"

"Nope. The matchmakers in town did it for him."

Emily could relate. She still had the phony lease in her briefcase for a house that didn't exist. "That was pretty sneaky."

"Yes. But it all turned out better than I ever could have imagined. There's something about this town, I think. It's magical."

"That's odd. It's always been magically jinxed for me."

Hannah smiled. "Give us another chance. You might be pleasantly surprised."

A rusty pickup pulled into the yard. "Who's that?"

Hannah looked out the window and grinned. "Mildred and Opal Bagley. Sisters who married brothers. They're both widowed, and they run a boardinghouse in town. You're in for a treat now."

"I remember them. I didn't know they'd turned their place into a boardinghouse, though."

The widows came in the door bickering, stopping only long enough to reintroduce themselves and put more food in the refrigerator before they each plucked a baby out of Emily and Hannah's arms respectively.

"Oh, aren't they just precious," Opal said. "Took care of my twin granddaughters—that was some years back, but I know how much of a handful they can be. What one don't think of the other one does. Didn't make a bit of difference they were girls. Got into as

GAS"

E

REE
TS!

Play the

"LAS

3 FRE

FREE GIFTS!

1. Pull back all 3 tabs on th
   see what we have for you
   FREE!

2. Send back this card and y
   Romance® novels. These'
   U.S. and $5.25 each in Ca

3. There's no catch. You're
   nothing — ZERO — for y
   any minimum number of

4. The fact is, thousands of r
   the Harlequin Reader Serv
   delivery...they like getting
   they're available in stores.
   featuring author news, hor

5. We hope that after receivin
   subscriber. But the choice
   all! So why not take us up o
   You'll be glad you did!

FREE!
No Obligation to Buy!
No Purchase Necessary!

Play the

"LAS VEGAS" Game

PEEL BACK HERE ▶
PEEL BACK HERE ▶
PEEL BACK HERE ▶

YES! I have pulled back the 3 tabs. Please send me all the free Harlequin American Romance® books and the gift for which I qualify. I understand that I am under no obligation to purchase any books, as explained on the back and opposite page.

354 HDL DFR9

154 HDL DFSA
(H-AR-OS-11/01)

NAME (PLEASE PRINT CLEARLY)

ADDRESS

APT.# CITY

STATE/PROV. ZIP/POSTAL CODE

7	7	7	**GET 2 FREE BOOKS & A FREE MYSTERY GIFT!**
✿	✿	✿	**GET 2 FREE BOOKS!**
🍒	🍒	🍒	**GET 1 FREE BOOK!**
🔔	🔔	🔔	**TRY AGAIN!**

The Harlequin Reader Service® — Here's how it works:

Accepting your 2 free books and gift places you under no obligation to buy anything. You may keep the books and gift and return the shipping statement marked "cancel." If you do not cancel, about a month later we'll send you 4 additional novels and bill you just $3.80 each in the U.S., or $4.21 each in Canada, plus 25¢ shipping & handling per book applicable taxes if any.* That's the complete price and — compared to cover prices of $4.50 each in the U.S. and $5.25 each in Canada — it's quite a bargain! You may cancel at any time, but if you choose to continue, every month we'll send you 4 more books, which you may either purchase at the discount price or return to us and cancel your subscription.

*Terms and prices subject to change without notice. Sales tax applicable in N.Y. Canadian residents will be charged applicable provincial taxes and GST.

much trouble as a passel of boys and nearly ran my daughter ragged.''

''Well, that's a fine how-do-you-do,'' Mildred complained. ''Walk right through the door and scare poor Emily to death, borrowing trouble before it even finds her.'' Mildred inspected Emily's hands, commiserating over the loss of the acrylics. ''A shame,'' she said.

Opal sniffed. ''Some people don't have time to fuss with fingernails. Besides, with you running in there every week or so, Arletta's not suffering a bit over the loss in business.''

''There's nothing wrong with wanting nice fingernails.''

Opal glared at her sister. ''Hush up before you make our Emily here feel self-conscious.''

Emily didn't feel a bit self-conscious about her lack of nails and was charmed right down to her toes by the two sisters. They bickered and cooed and managed to start a pot of tea and set out a plate of cookies, all the while holding the babies.

The women had thirty years on her and could run circles around her. She tried not to let that dent her pride.

''I was ready to give my hands a breather, anyway,'' she said, glancing down at her rough nails.

''Well, anytime you want to run into the beauty shop for a little pampering, you just drop these sweet babies off with us,'' Mildred said. ''We've got two laps and four arms between us and would love to sit.''

''Thank you.'' The women were the quintessential grandmothers, and Emily thought about her own mother, felt her heart sting. Tamara should have been here, cradling her grandchildren, experiencing the wonder and innocence of these two little lives.

Instead, loving strangers were providing the support normally reserved for family.

"Lord, would you look at that man!"

Emily, followed by Hannah and Mildred, joined Opal at the window, and Emily felt her heart kick into overdrive.

"If I was thirty years younger..." Mildred said, cradling Hunter as though she held babies every day. Her tone and her words were very *un*grandmotherly. "That's one tall drink of water, if you ask me."

Opal snorted and Hannah smothered a laugh. Emily drooled right along with Mildred as she gazed at Cheyenne sitting atop a horse.

She found it curious that he bought and sold mustangs, yet he rode a flashy paint-splashed chestnut.

He was incredible. Unique.

A warrior.

She wasn't sure why that image had popped into her mind. It was in his attitude, she supposed, the quiet, understated demeanor shaped by his past.

With the winter sun in his face, boots in the stirrups, reins held loosely in his gloved hands, he was a man who seemed at one with the land.

Lonely perhaps.

But the laid-back attitude was deceptive, Emily knew. Despite the gun he normally wore on his hip

and the star pinned to his chest, this man was dangerous.

Dangerous to her peace of mind.

Especially when she started thinking about him as
her true husband. A husband for keeps.

Chapter Eight

Cheyenne came to a halt at the bathroom door, astonished, amused...charmed.

Emily was posing in front of the mirror, her mouth pursed as though she were a teenager practicing kissing skills, her lips coated in cherry-red lipstick, slick and wet-looking. They'd been living in close quarters for several weeks now, and he still got a jolt every time he saw her in his home.

As he watched, she parted her lips, licked them, her eyes going soft and sensual as though a lover looked back at her through the reflection.

A lover who'd just asked a question.

And received a very carnal, very affirmative answer in return.

Desire slammed through him, making him hard in an instant.

Hell on fire, he wanted to be the man asking that question, asking for the go-ahead.

And he wanted her to look at him just like that, give him that answer, that ecstasy her lips and gaze promised.

He must have made a noise. Her gaze shifted. Then she literally jumped and gave a feminine, one-note scream.

"Oh, my gosh! How long have you been standing there?"

"Long enough."

Her face was nearly as bright as the lipstick on her incredibly full lips.

"I'm, uh...working."

He raised a brow. "Need any help?"

She gaped at him for a moment, then let out her breath in a whoosh. "I'm so embarrassed."

"No need. What are you working on?" He let his gaze travel down the rest of her, taking in her flannel nightshirt and thermal leggings. Not the most seductive outfit, by any means. To Cheyenne's way of thinking, it was hands-down better than a baby-doll negligee.

"A lipstick ad."

"Going for the sex angle, hmm?"

Her gaze touched on everything in the bathroom except him. "Sort of. Did you need in here?"

He shook his head. "You left the door open. I didn't mean to invade your privacy, but nothing'll stop a man quicker than a woman puckering her lips."

She brushed by him. "You've got to stop talking like that."

He followed her down the hall and into the kitchen. She had her laptop computer set up on the table. Faxes with drawings and memos were strewn amongst bottles, pacifiers, disposable diapers, baby powder and a cup of coffee gone cold.

"Talking like what?" he asked, knowing exactly what she meant. He didn't know why he kept baiting her. They had no business kissing—or thinking about it. She'd made it clear enough that they were supposed to be roommates.

Married roommates taking care of babies.

His mind kept refusing to remember the rules.

She clicked the computer's mouse on a drawing— lips, he noted—and dragged the image until it was larger, more pouty.

"Like about kissing."

"Did I say anything about kissing?"

She gave him a look as though he'd gone daft. It was an expression he imagined that had account executives falling in line. Even though she sat there in what appeared to be her pajamas, she still managed to look regal and commanding.

And had his hormones in a tangled mess.

"How are the kids?" It might be wise to change the subject.

"They're asleep—for the next two minutes at least—and I thought I'd take advantage of the time."

He noted the dark circles under her eyes and wished he could erase them. He had an idea his own were in the same shape. Between the kids and thoughts of Emily keeping him up nights, he was a zombie.

He pulled out a chair and sat at the table, watching as she fussed with the images on the screen, changing the shape, the color, the angle.

Hell, even her work evoked sexual images. So much for changing the subject.

He rose and poured them each a fresh cup of coffee, set hers at her elbow.

"Thanks," she said distractedly. "I can't seem to get this right."

"So you practice on yourself in the mirror?"

She shrugged, tucked a stray strand of hair behind her ear. "I have an image in my mind, but I can't get it to gel. These computers are amazing, but..."

"But what?"

She abandoned the computer and grabbed a sketch pad, casting a quick glance at the clock. He could tell she was under the gun, worried about the kids waking up, wanting to cram as much work as she could into the short amount of time.

That in itself was probably frustrating her.

"Jimmy would have drawn this in minutes. He was incredibly talented. It was as though he read my mind, captured my ideas perfectly."

Cheyenne took the sketch pad from her fingers, surprising her. "Tell me your ideas and let me see what I can do."

"You draw?"

"I can manage stick people, maybe a horse or two."

Emily laughed. "I need more than stick people."

He was watching her, the shading pencil in his hands moving across the paper. She couldn't see what he was doing.

"You going to tell me your idea?"

She knew this would set her back in terms of time,

but she just couldn't get herself too worked up about it. He was mouthwatering handsome sitting there, his dark eyes glancing up at her every so often. Probably wondering if she was waiting to laugh at his efforts with the pencil.

Since he wasn't working, he wasn't in his sheriff's uniform, but rather his cowboy one. A flannel shirt—unbuttoned now that he was indoors—with a thermal one beneath it that molded his chest like ink on glossy card stock.

His stomach muscles were rippled and hard as a rock—she'd touched them, so she should know—and were visible beneath the tight shirt.

She probably shouldn't be dwelling on the excellent parts of his anatomy, especially since she was the one who'd just taken him to task for baiting her about kissing.

"Emily?"

The ideas. *Pay attention, Emily.*

What the heck. Maybe she'd be pleasantly surprised. Maybe artistic ability ran in the family.

Focusing inward, she licked her lips. "Obviously I'm going for the sexual appeal of the lips. We're advertising lipstick. The kind that stays put."

He nodded, settled his gaze on her lips for a long moment before he transferred his attention back to the sketch pad. "Doesn't kiss off. Did you like the pouty pose or the one with slightly open mouth?"

"The one…" Good grief. She and Jimmy had done just this sort of thing countless times, bantered back and forth for clarification, but she'd never felt so flushed and fluttery with him.

"You know," Cheyenne coached, "the one with the mouth barely open, the eyes heavy, the look of anticipation, of yearning."

"Um...yes." Had she worn such a look when he'd caught her in the bathroom? "Maternal."

His pencil paused. "Excuse me?"

She cleared her throat. "I'm not sure where that came from. It's an idea I've been toying with lately." Ever since Cheyenne and two exhausting—yet precious—babies had come into her life.

His pencil started moving again. "Go on."

"As I said, I want to capture the sexual appeal of the lips and balance that subliminally with family. You know, like maybe it began with a kiss, sensual, sexy, burning, then sweetened into courtship and love, settled into marriage and children. The perfect family." Her voice was husky, dreamy. "And all it took was a kiss."

Emily realized the kitchen had gone silent—Cheyenne had gone silent. A horse nickered out in the barn. Wind batted the windows. The coffeepot puffed out steam like an afterthought.

She dragged herself out of the vivid image in her mind, focused on him.

His hands were still, his fingers gripping the pencil, his dark eyes intense as he stared at her.

Intense and filled with heat and something else she couldn't define.

He closed his fist around the page, crumpled it, then

stood and tossed it in the trash. ''Guess you're back to the drawing board. I can't do this justice. I'll be out in the barn for a bit. Pick up the phone and punch in the intercom if you need me.''

Without buttoning his flannel shirt, he shrugged into his coat, jammed his hat on his head and let himself out the kitchen door, a blast of cold air swirling in, carrying snowflakes onto the wood floor.

Stunned, Emily sat there for a minute. What in the world? She got up slowly and reached into the trash to retrieve the wadded-up paper, flattened it out against the counter.

Her breath caught.

Cheyenne was more than a passable artist. He didn't have the dramatic flair that Jimmy did, but his simple style was above average.

His strength, it appeared, was in capturing expressions.

And he'd captured hers. The likeness was amazing, though he'd smoothed out the rough edges some. She was certain she didn't look this relaxed and dewy-eyed.

Rather than frames that would eventually mesh together as a whole picture for advertising purposes, he'd done a portrait.

And in the portrait were a man and a woman, each holding an infant wrapped in a blanket. The woman's lips were parted, lush. Her expression was soft, maternal even, yet filled with a shining sensuality that made Emily feel a bit like a voyeur just looking at it.

The man in the sketch looked remarkably like Chey-

enne, yet he wore a hat that shaded his face and his
expression, his head tipped over his family as though
shielding them under the brim of his protection.

It was a portrait of them—Cheyenne, Emily and the
babies.

Her hands trembled as she ran her fingers over the
shading, smudging the lines a bit.

When she'd come up with the idea, she'd had older
kids in mind—actually just one child. A little girl playing dress-up with Mom's lipstick, Dad smiling down
at his two women.

She'd thought she was looking at the marketing angle of the idea. Little girls loved to play dress-up. Men
and women loved to kiss. She'd created an idea that
involved a loving family.

A Freudian slip perhaps? An ad that catered to the
sex appeal of a woman, as well as her maternal side,
showing that the two can and do mix?

And from her description, Cheyenne had drawn
them. She hadn't billed herself as the heroine of the
ad, yet here she was, in charcoal shading that captured
her right down to the uneven arch of her left brow,
the kinky curls that frizzed at her temples no matter
how much she tried to tame them.

And the man in the portrait. Oh, she knew that man,
could picture him. He was the bad boy with the gentle
streak. The guy who could kiss wildly, with the soul-
stealing rigor of youth. The guy with deep emotions
that he kept hidden, yet whose very silence and mystery would draw a young girl like a moth batting at a
flame. The guy who fought and clawed for respect-

ability, who'd tamed the wild streak of youth, mellowed with maturity, harnessed his sensuality into something explosive that only time and experience could accomplish, tempered it with a gentle touch and protective streak.

The kind of guy who knew where he'd been and where he was headed, who would always be there for his family.

The kind of guy who gave his love only once, and it was forever.

Cheyenne Bodine.

Her husband.

Emily pressed a hand to her heart, felt the dampness that had seeped through the nursing pads in her bra.

She blinked. "Good grief. Get a grip."

Taking a breath, she folded the paper and tucked it into her attaché case.

It might be in the wrong format, might not be commercial-quality graphics, but if she faxed this drawing to the company's media buyer—who just happened to be a woman—the Cockran agency would get the account for sure.

Women around the world would buy the lipstick just to dream about the man.

The problem was, this man wasn't someone Emily wanted exploited. She didn't want to share him.

The drawing was too personal.

And the fact that she realized that told her she was in deep, deep trouble.

HALF-ASLEEP AND DEAD on her feet, Emily stared at both babies, who were squalling as though their little hearts were broken.

"Alicia, right?" she said as she lifted one baby. She peered inside the diaper. "Got it on the first try. Do me a favor, will you, sweetie pie? Don't even think of dieting. Chubby cheeks are all the rage and you're beautiful just the way you are."

"And so's her mom."

Emily whirled around. She'd known Cheyenne would come when he heard the babies cry, so she shouldn't have been surprised to see him there.

But she was, just the same. He stood silhouetted by the dim hall light, shirtless, shoeless, his jeans unsnapped. And in his large hand, he held a bottle.

The sight was so sexy she nearly sighed.

Her gaze went to that washboard stomach and she felt her heart flutter.

Her hormones had very poor timing.

Alicia was nuzzling at her chest, snuffling, managing to get her thumb in her mouth. Finding that it had nothing she wanted, she fussed and fidgeted. So much that she nearly wriggled out of Emily's hold.

And Hunter, obviously responding to his sister's distress, joined in like a good sibling.

Emily turned a beseeching gaze back to Cheyenne, wondering if she looked as wild-eyed and dazed as she felt.

"He need a diaper change first?"

"Naturally. They both do."

Cheyenne moved to the crib the babies were sharing, and he and Emily worked side by side, unsnapping footed pajamas, extracting fragile little legs, cooing and soothing to no avail.

Emily was sweating by the time she got the tapes of the diapers in place, and had to try three times to get the snaps of the pajamas to line up.

"Shush, baby." She tried to make her voice soothing, but it sounded more like she was begging. She sat down in the rocking chair and draped a blanket over her shoulder, wincing as Alicia finally latched on to her breast.

Cheyenne lifted Hunter and sat down in the second rocking chair, easing the bottle into the infant's mouth. After a few weak cries and snuffling noises, Hunter quieted and settled down to eat.

It amazed her how easy and comfortable she felt with Cheyenne. At first she'd been self-conscious nursing in front of him, even though she always made sure to cover herself. But over the past two weeks, this had become a nightly ritual—more than nightly actually.

When the world was quiet like this, in the deep of the night, with the wind batting softly at the windows, the sharing felt special. Intimate in a nonsexual way.

It was only when her fantasies kicked in and her mind strayed that the intimacy took on a sexual feel.

She rocked and studied the man across from her. The baby wasn't even as long as Cheyenne's forearm. As he gazed down at the child he cradled, Emily let herself look her fill. The sight of him holding Hunter so gently, so lovingly, moved her.

The perfect advertisement for fatherhood. Or for bottles, or formula. Diapers, perhaps.

Strength and innocence. Large and small. Nothing was more moving than a shirtless, virile man gently cradling an infant against his wide, bare chest.

He looked up, caught her staring.

"What?" he whispered.

"Just thinking about advertising."

"Work's never far from your mind, is it."

"It's been my life."

"And you're good at it."

She nodded. There was no conceit. Just confidence. "Advertising I'm good at. Babies are another matter." She stroked Alicia as she spoke, noticed that Cheyenne did the same with Hunter. He used only his thumb, rubbing it from shoulder to fingertip of Hunter's arm, his hand nearly as big as the child's body.

She wondered if he knew that touch and massage would cause a baby to grow faster. She'd learned that on the Internet when she'd been researching everything she could think of that had to do with babies.

"You're doing fine," he said softly.

"Sometimes I wonder. When they cry, I go into a tizzy. They're so precious, Cheyenne. But they can't talk. They can't tell me what they need. I worry that I won't know. That I'll do something wrong."

"You have incredible instincts," he said. "You'll know what they need."

"How can you be so sure?"

He rocked in silence for a few minutes, adjusted the

bottle in Hunter's mouth. Blue padded into the room and lay down beside Cheyenne's chair, a faithful friend.

"Remember when we were kids and you shared your sandwich with me?"

For a minute her mind went blank, then an image slowly crystallized like storyboard frames in perfect order: outdoor tables scarred by weather and use at the back of the schoolhouse; she, an underdeveloped four-teen-year-old, he, a sexy, sullen seventeen-year-old who seemed far older than his years. And in his eyes, there had been a hunger that went much deeper than an empty belly. "Yes, I remember."

"You knew what I needed."

"That's different. You could talk."

"But I didn't."

No, he hadn't. He'd just sat there, alone, apart from everyone else, pretending he didn't care, his expression closed, daring anyone to comment or approach him. Most of the kids had enough self-preservation to respect his barriers. Emily had simply led with her heart and was across the schoolyard before she'd thought better of it. She knew what it was like to be teased, to be talked about, to be the underdog.

She was amazed that he remembered the incident, surprised it had made enough of an impact on him for him to bring it up this many years later.

"I was a little afraid of you," she admitted. "But very intrigued."

He stared at her. For one heartbeat, then two. "And I was half in love with you."

Her heart leaped even though she knew he didn't mean it literally.

She needed to say something so her mind wouldn't run off on a wild tangent that could only cause her heartache.

"Yes, I'm sure a skinny little flat-chested girl with freckles and pigtails filled you with lust." She wasn't flat-chested anymore and she saw his gaze dip to her breasts—which he couldn't see because of the blanket she had draped across herself.

"You had grit."

Oh, she liked that. Grit got you places in the world.

"And a heart as big as the open prairie," he added.

For some reason, that made her uncomfortable. In business, a big heart could get you stepped on, make a woman miss a rung of the ladder. Emily had made it a point not to miss too many of those rungs.

"I don't know why you keep trying to make me out to be such a softy. That's not me."

"You don't call a surrogate mother a softy?"

"No. That was love."

"And love's not soft?"

"Well, yes. But it was slotted, you know?" How did she explain? "A softy ends up giving up a lot. I wasn't giving up anything. I could do my job, keep my life and still give my sister her dream."

But it hadn't worked out that way. And her explanation didn't sound so cut-and-dried when she voiced it in the quiet of the night like this, with the wind blowing snow against the windows, Cheyenne cradling a baby in his arms and she with another at her breast.

"I take my responsibilities seriously, Cheyenne. Don't try to read more into me than is there." Was he hoping she could give him more? She didn't want to hurt him. She had a job she loved, one she intended to go back to. The children would go with her, and of course there would be changes in her life, but she would manage. She always had.

Without dislodging the blanket, she brought Alicia out from under it and raised her to her shoulder, patting the little back gently to coax a burp. Milk dribbled from the corner of the baby's mouth, leaving a saliva trail across her chubby cheeks. Emily kissed that soft, warm cheek, inhaling the essence of the child, her heart turning over.

They might be a handful, but she loved these babies more than she'd ever thought possible.

"Trade," she said to Cheyenne.

He tugged the bottle out of Hunter's mouth, burped him, then rose and laid him in Emily's arm, carefully taking Alicia from her shoulder. She liked to try to nurse both babies at each feeding, wanting to cement the bond between her and them equally. She truly was afraid that one of the babies would end up being slighted, and she nearly ran herself ragged trying to avoid it.

"Tell me about my brother."

"What do you want to know?"

"What was he like, how did he spend his days, anything and everything you can think of." He stroked a finger over Alicia's cheek. She was sucking at the same bottle her brother had moments ago. "Show me the man I didn't get to know."

Emily focused inward, recalling Jimmy's blond hair and handsome features as though he stood right there in the room with them.

"When he came into the agency looking for a job, he didn't have an appointment, but he was so darn charming I told him I'd give him five minutes to make his pitch."

Cheyenne nodded. "As a kid he could wrap folks around his finger without half trying."

"Yes, he was good at that. He'd gone to a trade school and gotten a certificate in graphic arts. We usually hired artists who had a full degree, but one look at Jimmy's portfolio and I knew he had talent. I hired him on the spot. He wasn't afraid of work. He was the first one there in the morning and the last one to leave. Sometimes I had to threaten him to get him to go home."

"Where was home?"

"An apartment in the city at first. When he and Debbie got married, they bought a pretty condo overlooking Puget Sound. He loved sports—especially basketball—and he came up with some wildly successful ad campaigns with sports themes. He shied away from alcohol ads."

"Our parents were drinkers."

"Yes, he told me." Because the memory seemed to make Cheyenne sad, she moved on. "He proposed to Debbie at a SuperSonics game. Had 'I love you, Debbie. Will you marry me?' flashed on the scoreboard at Seattle Center.''

"You were there with them?"

"Yes. I still have the game ball. All the players signed it as a wedding gift."

"That'll mean a lot to Hunter one of these days."

"Shame on you. What about Alicia? Girls can be just as devoted to sports as boys."

"I stand ashamed."

He stroked Alicia's downy head. It still amazed her how he could hold the baby and the bottle with one hand and leave the other free. She had yet to accomplish that feat.

He'd gone silent on her, and she had an idea he was thinking about all that he'd missed in his brother's life. Because Jimmy had been the one to bounce between his divorced parents, staying with his father most of the time, then striking out on his own, Emily likely had more memories than Cheyenne did.

It was sad. And she could tell it bothered him. Because Cheyenne was a man who obviously yearned for family. He might not openly admit it, but his actions spoke for him.

"He was happy, then?" Cheyenne asked.

"Yes. These last three years, he truly was. He regretted rebuffing you when you tried to make amends that last time. I think he was afraid that if he opened the lines of communication with you, he'd become weak, want to depend on you."

"He never depended on me."

"Yes, he did. More than you knew. He idolized

you. But he felt responsible for your father, and he ended up getting sucked into the wrong crowd. He told me there were several years where he wasn't such a nice person. I guess after your father died and that incident between the two of you occurred, he hit bottom.''

Cheyenne rested his head against the back of the rocker and closed his eyes. ''I let him down.''

''No. Actually he said you did him a favor, that if you'd bailed him out, he probably would've kept screwing up. I never knew that side of him. By the time he'd applied for the job at the agency, he'd gotten some education, mellowed into a quiet, intensely driven man.''

''Why didn't he contact me?''

''I think he was afraid at first. He didn't trust his new strength, didn't want to put it to the test. Sort of like an alcoholic fears his first party after sobriety, I think. Jimmy was a perfectionist, in his job and in his life. I didn't know the boy, but the man was careful and thorough, and he thought long and hard about each step, determined to get it right. Except when it came to my sister.''

''She bewitched him?''

Emily nodded, shared his smile. ''From the moment they laid eyes on each other, they were hooked.'' It had been a beautiful thing to watch. Because her own parents hadn't had a happily-ever-after, Emily had stopped believing in the fairy tale. She'd almost changed her emotional belief system when she'd seen her sister's happy marriage, but then death had intervened.

But watching that relationship develop so quickly and genuinely, she'd allowed herself to dream just a little, had started to wonder if perhaps there was indeed one true love for everyone, wondered if she'd recognize him instantly if that special person came along for her.

She gazed at Cheyenne, so silent, so gentle, so strong and giving. Was it the stress of all that was going on in her life that made her entertain the crazy thought that Cheyenne Bodine might just be that special person for her?

Her heart pounded and her palms went damp. She told herself to just stop it. Their relationship was because of the babies. It was the equivalent of the survival theory, where the one being rescued mixed up feelings of gratitude and love for the rescuer.

And Cheyenne, in essence, had come to her rescue.

She had to remember that. Her life was in Washington. Not on a peaceful mustang ranch with a sexy sheriff who made her hormones sing and her insides burn.

Chapter Nine

Emily stood beside the bed and stared down at her lopsided breasts. Was there no end to the horrors of her body?

It had been two and a half weeks since she'd given birth to the twins, yet she had so much flab and sag it was appalling. Her clothes didn't come close to fitting, so she had to wear baggy stuff—zippers were still entirely out of the question.

And now this.

One bosom the size of a plump cantaloupe, the other drooping like an underfilled water balloon. Thirty-two years old and her chest had already gone south. And deformed at that.

She added extra cotton pads in the left side. Good grief, she hadn't stuffed her bra since junior high.

Between nursing and pumping, she kept forgetting which side she was using most. Iris had suggested safety pins in the bra as a marker. But she could hardly remember her own name, much less to stick a pin in her bra.

"I'm just a regular sex goddess," she muttered.

Cheyenne cleared his throat, scaring her to death, making her whirl around. Too late she realized she was standing in her unbecoming stretch pants and huge nursing bra.

Lopsided bra.

She snatched a towel off the end of the bed and held it up. "Good grief."

"You should close the door."

"And you should be a gentleman and not come in. Besides, if I close the door, I can't hear the kids."

"Who told you I was a gentleman?"

He was in an odd mood this morning, and it made her nervous. He'd been doing that a lot lately. Teasing her. Baiting her. Then there was that incident the other day with the drawing, when he'd gone all silent on her and taken himself off to the barn.

It was becoming more difficult to judge his mood, to get a bead on him.

"I wanted to know if you need anything from town."

"Are you going in to work today?"

"For a couple of hours. Some of the neighbors are going to come over and check on you."

She felt such relief, and hated it. She still didn't trust herself to be all alone with the kids. She was getting better with them, but the fears were still there.

Hoping to arm herself with knowledge, thus allaying some of her nerves, she'd logged on to the Internet and researched everything she could on babies and parenthood.

That information-gathering spree probably had

something to do with why one bosom was so much smaller than the other. She'd likely pumped it dry. But the articles she'd read had expounded on the benefits of mother's milk in the first weeks of a child's life. Emily wanted to give Debbie's children every advantage. And she'd found that using the breast pump didn't hurt the way it did when the twins nursed at her breasts. She didn't understand it, but there it was.

She might be overdoing it, though, and thought she ought to call Kelly Anderson or Chance and make sure.

"I can't think of anything I need right now. The neighbors have brought enough food to last us six months."

Emily realized she wouldn't be here for six months.

But Cheyenne would.

Eating casseroles alone.

"You okay?"

How did he read her so well? Was she such an open book that her emotions showed on her face?

"I'm fine. Getting a little cold standing here behind this towel."

He grinned. "Sorry to intrude. It's tough to pass by an open door when you're in the room, though. I'd hate to miss another of those kissing rehearsals."

Her face heated and she had a very real urge to throw her hairbrush at him. Instead, she gathered her dignity around her—or as much of it as she could, given the fact that she was standing here with a thin bath sheet shielding lopsided breasts, an unbecoming nursing bra and a nonexistent waistline that still hung over the waistband of her stretch pants.

"Go to work, Cheyenne. You're making me a nervous wreck."

He grinned. "I'm going." He started to move out of the doorway, stopped. "Emily?"

She was still holding her breath. "What?"

"I agree."

She stared at him, thoroughly lost.

"Definitely a sex goddess."

She had to sit down. Because even though his tone was teasing, his eyes were not. He really thought she was sexy.

Good grief!

What in the world had gotten into the man?

This hadn't been part of the bargain.

THE BABIES WERE AWAKE and cooing, instead of crying, by the time Cheyenne came home from work.

Progress, Emily decided. Figures, though, that they'd show their best manners to Cheyenne. He'd probably think they'd been this angelic all day—which they definitely had not.

But, oh, these times when they cooed and waved their little arms around, blowing spit bubbles and blinking owl-like eyes up at her, were priceless.

She glanced up and frowned when Cheyenne banged something against the door. Why didn't the man just come in? Couldn't he see that he was letting the cold in and the warmth out?

"Shut the door, for heaven's sake!"

"I'm trying."

Her eyes widened when she saw why he was struggling. In one hand he carried a spongy football and a rag doll. The other was pushing a deluxe-model double stroller designed for twins.

"Hmmm," was all Emily said, yet she smiled.

He shrugged, looking sheepish. Which wasn't at all like him.

"I was over in south county and the store was close. I figured you'd be needing one of these pretty soon."

She felt her heart give an apprehensive kick. "I don't think I'm up to outings just yet."

"Well, it's here when you're ready. So what do you think?"

"Looks pretty fancy."

"Top of the line," he said proudly. "They had a pretty cool remote-control car, but I resisted. Didn't want the kids to fight."

"They're already fighting. Alicia bashed Hunter in the head with her fist." Never mind that the baby didn't have any motor skills to speak of in order to take deliberate aim. Hunter had cried as though he'd been mortally wounded, and Alicia had joined in, apology or commiseration, Emily couldn't tell which.

"Violence," Cheyenne said with a weary grin. "What's the world coming to?"

She looked more closely at him. He seemed tired. "Bad day?"

He went into the kitchen and poured himself a cup of coffee, then brought it back out into the living room. She'd noticed he never drank alcohol—or at least he hadn't since she'd been here.

"Domestic-battery call. A family out by the reservation. I can't tell you how many times I've removed the husband from the house. But the wife won't press charges and he always returns."

"And you're called back out."

He nodded, set his cup on the coffee table and eased himself to the floor where she sat next to the babies. Lying on a thick blanket close to the warmth of the fireplace, both infants were churning their legs and arms.

He stretched out beside them, propped on his elbow, stroking his fingers over each baby as though to assure himself that they hadn't changed in the hours he'd been gone.

Alicia latched on to his finger, managed to get it in her mouth. He smiled at the unladylike sucking sound she made.

"She hungry?"

"She's always hungry. I fed them both a couple of hours ago—which doesn't mean a whole lot. They don't seem to be attached to any sort of reasonable schedule."

"Mmm. And you're a woman who likes schedules."

"Well, yes. Organization at least."

Little of that prevailed in the house. The living room had been unintentionally transformed by a new decorating scheme. A box of diapers sat on the end table, along with lotion and powder. An empty bottle rested on its side on the sofa. Rattles and pacifiers were strewn on the blanket the babies lay on.

It was all very domestic—if a little messy.

Firelight reflected off the star pinned to Cheyenne's chest. A shiver of worry crawled beneath her skin. He'd mentioned a domestic-violence call. Those kind were the most dangerous for law-enforcement officials, weren't they? Cheyenne was such a confident, competent man she hadn't given much thought to the dangers of his profession.

"Do you like your job?" she asked.

His brown eyes met hers. "Yes, most of the time."

"I don't imagine there's much crime in Shotgun Ridge."

"My territory covers the whole county. But you're right. This is a great town, peaceful. The Bagley widows have a tendency to call us out to settle squabbles—but I think that's more for the entertainment of their guests."

Emily laughed. "I've witnessed their 'entertainment.' They're delightful. Isn't the boardinghouse right across the street from the station?"

"Yes." He grinned. "That's what makes it so convenient. They have an uncanny knack of knowing when we're not busy."

"More likely because they can see in your windows."

"Mmm. Did the neighbors come help you out today?"

"Yes. Dora came over this morning and Eden this afternoon. They're both so calm around the kids."

"They've had practice. I didn't mean to leave you so long."

"That's okay. You brought gifts." She grinned. "Besides, I've got to wean myself from total dependency pretty soon."

He glanced away, stared at the fire, his finger still clutched in Alicia's tiny fist. She couldn't tell what he was thinking.

Perhaps the same thing she was—that once she "weaned" herself from dependence on others, it would be time to go. She was on maternity leave through January. Time enough to worry about that.

Looking closer, she decided his preoccupation went deeper.

"The woman you helped today, the one with the nasty husband—she's someone you know, isn't she?" Emily could tell he was still keyed up. She had an urge to reach across the blanket, to run her fingers through his dark hair, push back that stubborn lock that kept falling forward. To soothe him.

"I dated her years ago. She's my age, but she looks closer to fifty-five than thirty-five."

"Do you still have feelings for her?"

"Not in the way you mean. But nobody should have to put up with that kind of treatment. It baffles me why she won't leave, why she keeps letting him come back. I've talked to her till I'm blue in the face. She won't meet my eyes. Just cowers. It makes my gut twist in knots." His chest rose and fell on a long tired breath. "I'm waiting for the day I have to call out the coroner, instead of the paramedics."

She did reach out then and covered his hand. He turned it over, linked his fingers with hers, stroked her knuckles with his thumb, much the same way he'd stroked Hunter's arm when he'd been feeding him— absently, gently.

"You're a good man, Cheyenne."

His gaze shifted from their joined hands to her eyes, held. "Just doing my job."

She had an idea he was repeating a variation of her own words, but she didn't understand what he might be trying to tell her.

Did he regret the sacrifices he'd made for his job? The sacrifices that cost him his relationship with Jimmy?

But Jimmy had caused the rift between them by breaking the law, asking his brother to abet the crime. That wasn't right.

Or was he subtly reiterating how he saw her? Putting her up on a pedestal she didn't deserve? He wanted her to believe she was some sort of heroine. For what? Accepting responsibility? Loving two little babies, more and more with each breath she took? He was doing the same.

"We're a fine pair, aren't we?"

"We could be." He said it softly, seriously.

And Emily's heart fluttered in panic.

"Your coffee's getting cold," she said, and hopped to her feet. "I'll just warm it up for you." She was running away and didn't know why. *Liar.*

CHEYENNE FELT A SENSE of déjà vu as he turned into his driveway. Packed snow crunched under the knobby tires of the Bronco, furrowing ruts in its wake.

Blue sat beside him on the seat, ears perked and alert. He often took the dog to work with him when he figured it'd be a slow day. On the days it wasn't so slow, Blue was like a partner to him. Well trained, the dog could be docile as a lamb or fierce and threatening. Sometimes a menacing growl from the husky was more effective than a pointed gun.

"Now, who do you suppose is driving that trendy little car?" The Volvo was a rental, he noted, from an outfit over in Billings.

Since Cheyenne hadn't expected company to come calling in a rental car, he figured it must be one of Emily's friends. Thanksgiving was two days away. Had she invited someone special to share it with them?

Uneasiness assailed him for no good reason.

"Come on, boy. Let's go see what's up." Out of habit, he pushed the driver's side door closed with hardly a sound.

With his hat dripping melted snow, he stopped in the mudroom. His kitchen had been transformed into what looked like an advertising boardroom—though he'd never seen one firsthand, his imagination was in fine working order.

The ordered chaos didn't distress him nearly as much as the handsome young yuppie-type leaning over Emily, one hand touching her shoulder with a familiarity that made Cheyenne's gut twist, his other hand gesturing expansively to the storyboards propped on every available surface.

Blue shook to dislodge the snow from his coat, and his tags jingled.

Emily looked up with a smile. Cheyenne felt a little better. The smile was genuine. A welcome.

And he was being an idiot. If he wasn't sure it was such a ludicrous idea, he'd think he was jealous.

"Cheyenne. Come meet Dave Kimble. We work together at Cockran Advertising. Dave just flew in today. Dave, this is Cheyenne Bodine," she said.

The pretty boy in khaki slacks and a casual sport shirt moved forward to shake hands. "Pleased to meet you. Em tells me you're Jimmy's brother. Sorry to hear about the accident. Jimmy was a good man."

"Thank you." Em, was it? Not Emily, or Ms. Vincent, or Mrs. Bodine, for that matter. Very familiar.

"I hope you don't mind us taking over your kitchen this way. Faxes are great, but sometimes a project needs a hands-on approach."

Yeah, and if this guy didn't keep his hands to himself and stop touching Emily after every third word, Cheyenne was going to get pretty ticked off. As it was, he tucked his hands in his pockets, casually brushing aside his jacket so that his uniform shirt, badge and gun belt were visible. Hell, he hadn't done this kind of strutting since he was a puffed-up deputy sheriff still wet behind the ears and full of his own power.

"I don't mind," he said slowly. "It's Emily's kitchen, as well."

"Yes, she mentioned about the mixup in addresses. It's good of you to put her up this way."

Well, she'd been a regular font of information,

hadn't she. Just how close were these two? And why the hell did he care?

"Will we be putting you up, too?"

Dave laughed. "No. I've booked a room in town at the boardinghouse. Quaint thing, that. Didn't know those places were still around. This town's like walking into a Norman Rockwell painting. I've got to say, those two widows are delightful. The one with the Christmas trees painted on her fingernails actually hit on me."

"Mildred," Cheyenne and Emily said at the same time. They both smiled. Then Cheyenne turned back to Dave.

"So, you work with my wife."

"I do?" Baffled, Dave looked from Emily to Cheyenne. His brows shot upward toward his perfectly groomed sandy hair. "You're...you two are married?"

Emily nodded and Cheyenne kept his features bland as she glared at him. He wasn't quite sure where this dog-in-the-manger behavior had come from and felt a little ashamed. And he damned sure didn't want to admit it had hurt that Emily hadn't mentioned their marriage to her associate.

Then again, why should she have? It wasn't as though it was a real marriage.

"I thought you were just having babies, Em. Just on maternity leave."

"I hardly had a chance to say anything," she said to Dave. "You dumped the smiling toilet tissue, macho-man exterminator and the cosmetics ad on me before I could even draw a decent breath.''

"Sorry, kiddo," Dave said, easily dismissing the marriage subject when she reminded him of his work. Short attention span, Cheyenne thought. The man smiled, showing a fortune in dental work. "I was really excited about that smiling-toilet-paper idea.''

"Well, you can forget that one. I hate that ridiculous yellow happy face. It's been done to death.''

"You're kidding, right?'' Dave's expression fell as though she'd just maligned Santa Claus.

"Nope.'' As she spoke, she fielded babies, bottles and business.

Without any apparent thought that Cheyenne could see, she automatically passed one of the kids to him, along with a bottle, then plucked the other out of the infant seat and stuck a bottle in its mouth.

He checked the baby in his arms. Alicia. Her blue eyes were wide open and trained on him. He wanted to lose himself in the wonder of holding this child, but was too awed and astonished seeing Emily in action like this and, instead, focused on her.

She glanced at him to make sure he was doing his job with the feeding, then paced the room, Hunter in her arms, studying the boards that sat everywhere with all manner of drawings on them, dismissing him as though he wasn't there.

Or as though she trusted him and felt certain she didn't have to spend any time handing out instructions.

He adjusted the bottle that had slipped out of Alicia's mouth when he was paying attention to Emily, instead of what he was supposed to be doing.

She was always roping him in, it seemed. Marriage, dragging him into the labor and delivery, passing him kids to care for without so much as a "pretty please."

She really was efficient, though. She was handling both babies and business with relative ease, and he didn't think she even realized it. Her capabilities were so clear to onlookers and so *un*clear to her. She still doubted her abilities, worried she wasn't up to responsible tasks when it came to the kids.

It didn't make sense.

If she didn't *think* the process to death, she was just fine. It was when she allowed herself to dwell on things that she got scared. But with each day, she was getting better, more sure of herself.

On the one hand, Cheyenne cheered her on. On the other, the selfish part of him would mourn the loss of dependency she had on him, the way she beseeched him with those wide green eyes, the way her lips would part on a relieved sigh when he did nothing more than slip an arm around her, stand by her side, give her moral support.

And that line of thought was going to get him in trouble.

He noticed that she kept glancing in disapproval at the toilet-paper ad.

He was still a little peeved at the yuppie's familiarity and the fact that Emily hadn't mentioned having a husband, but at the moment he was inclined to join forces with this Dave person.

He wanted to know what in the wide world was wrong with the happy face.

He moved up next to her where she was examining a computer rendering of a beefy, muscle-bound character pointing a bug-spray can in the shape of a taser gun at a cowering insect.

"Nobody hates the happy face, trouble. That's practically un-American." They were standing side by side, each holding a baby sucking contentedly at their respective bottles.

She shrugged. "I know. And I just feel awful about it."

He felt his lips twitch. She truly sounded forlorn. "Is this a recent dislike or have you always had it in for the poor thing?"

"Oh, I love him in certain instances. There are computer happy faces with all manner of cute expressions, and I like him stamped on pages and stuff. I think it was when one of our competitors exploited him singing a song I personally detest that I got turned off."

"Mmm. Guess there's hope for you still. It's not the happy face you object to, it's the music."

"I have to turn off the TV set every time the ad airs."

"Seems to me, instead of dismissing him, you should give him back his dignity and remake him. Exploit him in a happier, cuddlier way."

She glanced over at the toilet-tissue boards, and he could see her mind working. Emily had always had a sharp mind. It was one of the things he admired most about her.

"That's sound advice," Dave said, glancing at the baby Emily held, but keeping his distance. "You remember that e-mail you showed me, the one with the happy faces with all the different expressions? Laughing, frowning, shocked. They were crazy. We can use that. Take your classic yellow ball here and open up the mouth, animate it."

"No singing," she warned.

"Of course not, boss. We'll go for innocent and cute, warm and fuzzy, like Cheyenne here suggested." Warming to his subject, Dave got into it, mimicking the expressions. "Oh, no," he sang dramatically. "Not that tissue. It's too scratchy!"

Emily laughed. "All right, all right. We'll work on it. But the gun in the bug-spray ad's got to go."

"Why?" Dave demanded, abandoning his absurd facial expressions.

"Because it conjures up images of violence."

"Killing bugs is violent business."

"We don't have to bash people over the head with the image. Kids will be watching."

"Kids see violence every day. Look at the video games, the comic books, for crying out loud."

"Cockran's name is not associated with those video games or comic books. I'll give you your happy face, Dave, but not the gun. Exaggerate the can, make the product label bigger, strain the muscles of the he-man exterminator and fan the spray out in a larger stream. Work on the bug, too. Don't make him so cute, covering his eyes like that with his legs. You'll have every kid and softhearted person in America feeling sorry for him and rooting for him. Toughen him up a bit. He's a nasty roach and he's moved into the kitchen and arrogantly thinks he owns the place. Balance his look between you-can't-hurt-me and uh-oh.''

She was good, Cheyenne thought. Damned good.

She thought of every angle, guarding young minds, tempering sympathy so it was allied on the right side, exploiting the main purpose of the advertising by giving the product name a focal point. She thought on her feet, was confident and quick.

She deserved the promotion she sought so desperately. This was her arena. This is where she belonged.

And seeing her in action this way, he knew she would never give it up.

Marriage license or not, Emily Vincent Bodine would indeed return to Washington when her maternity leave was at an end.

Chapter Ten

Thanksgiving dinner was at Eden and Stony Stratton's, and Cheyenne told her that half the town would probably show up since Eden was, hands down, the best cook in these parts. She'd given up a lucrative catering business in Texas when she'd come to Shotgun Ridge with health problems and a desperate need for a baby.

Eden herself had told Emily the story, and even now, Emily caught herself wanting to sigh. There were several beautiful love stories that had blossomed in this town.

"Last year at Thanksgiving, Dora fainted before dinner," Cheyenne said as he opened the back door of Emily's Mercedes to extract the twins. "Turns out she was newly pregnant with Ryan. Brought Ethan right to his knees. Not a sight we see often. Wonder what kind of excitement we'll have this year."

Emily just hoped the excitement wasn't caused by her. She was a little apprehensive about the whole affair, and because this was the first real outing she'd taken the twins on and also because she wasn't used to packing up children and baby paraphernalia, she'd started early, now she and Cheyenne were going to be the first to arrive.

Once again Emily hoped she wouldn't turn into a klutz or something.

Cheyenne moved up beside her, steadying her as she juggled Alicia. "I'll come back for the car seats, though I don't imagine we'll lack for arms to hold the babies." He studied her in that quiet, watchful way of his. "You okay?"

"Nervous," she admitted. "I have a tendency to blunder when I am in public—in this town. I'm hoping I don't do anything to give your neighbors reason to talk."

"Emily, everyone's crazy about you."

"Be that as it may, I had somewhat of a reputation for getting into trouble as a girl—although I swear I was innocent most of the time. And I've already managed to get on the wrong side of the law with that speeding ticket. I know you took some grief over it, because at least four people have mentioned the incident to me."

"I can handle harmless teasing. Look at me, trouble."

She lifted her gaze. In his eyes was amusement—and something more.

"You're my lady. That puts you on the right side of the law."

Her heart kicked into a fast beat. Emotions sizzled between them, bringing a flash of heat to the frigid November air. She was fairly certain if they hadn't had their hands full of infants, he'd have kissed her.

And she'd have let him.

She took a breath, filling her lungs with the scent of wood smoke and horses. "We should probably go in before the kids turn to icicles."

As it turned out, they weren't the first to arrive, after all. The four matchmakers were already there.

Ozzie Peyton, the town mayor and retired rancher, met them at the door. Behind him were Lloyd Brewer, owner of Brewer's Saloon, Vernon Tillis who ran the general store and Henry Jenkins of Jenkins Feed and Seed.

Emily wondered who was minding the stores, then remembered it was a holiday.

"Where are Iris and Vera?" Cheyenne asked, unshouldering two diaper bags while trying not to jostle the baby in his arms.

"Still baking up a batch of pies," Lloyd answered. He was a big, burly man with a full head of hair and a ruddy complexion. "They'll be along shortly."

"Eden's the expert baker," Vernon explained, "but the women insisted on pitching in. Don't imagine anybody'll complain none about the desserts, though. Iris and my Vera have won many a blue ribbon at the fairs for their pumpkin and apple pies."

Emily kept a smile on her face, but she felt just awful. She'd offered to bring a dish, but Eden had told her no. Should she have insisted as the other women apparently had?

Ozzie elbowed his way past his friends. "Well, let's have a look-see at these young'uns. Mighty fine-lookin' pair, you bet. Hand 'em over, why don't you.

Henry and I'll have a go, and Lloyd and Vern'll take the next turn. Give you kids a chance to relax, spend a little time without your arms so full.''

His vivid blue eyes twinkled. Emily had a feeling he was up to something. As matchmakers, they were less than subtle.

They'd barely transferred the babies into the old guys' arms when Mildred and Opal Bagley showed up, breezing through the door, patent-leather pocketbooks draped over their arms, wool coats buttoned to the neck, scarves in autumn colors draping their collars.

"Well, now," Opal said the minute she'd cleared the door and set down her covered dish. She tugged off her gloves. "We came early and a good thing, too. A bunch of old fools, the lot of you," she said, aiming the words at Ozzie. "Hand over that child before you drop her. Sister, get Hunter from Vernon. Honestly.''

"Now hold on just a dang minute," Ozzie objected, but relinquished the baby readily enough. No sense getting in a scuffle. "We've all plenty of experience with young'uns. Plenty in town lately, and we've all taken a turn with them. You bet.''

He glared at Opal. He'd hardly gotten a good feel of that little bundle. Telling him he didn't know how to hold a baby, he grumbled silently. Though he and his sweet Vanessa hadn't been blessed with little ones of their own, they'd been like surrogate parents to the rest of the children in town. And Vanessa, God rest her loving soul, had been the schoolteacher. Had the perfect disposition for mothering.

He figured that being the case—them practically adopting half her students—gave him more in common with Emily and Cheyenne.

More than either of these old bats cooing over the twins now.

On the other hand, he probably shouldn't be kicking up such a fuss. Never mind the Bagley widows were horning in on their matchmaking venture—he could tell by that sly, pleased look that passed between the sisters, and durned if his eyesight wasn't still twenty-twenty. At least they were all on the same page.

And now Cheyenne's arm was plenty free to drape around young Emily's shoulders if he was of a mind to do so. You bet. And if the boy didn't have the good sense to think of it on his own, well, they'd just figure out a way to give a little nudge.

"You just let us know when your arms get tired," he said to Mildred and Opal. "Me and the boys are perfectly capable of taking a turn."

"Shoo," Mildred said, flicking her painted fingernails at him. The woman had Christmas trees on her claws and they hadn't even carved the Thanksgiving turkey yet. "You men go watch a football game or something. Grab hold of the remote before those Callahan boys get here."

She had a good point. Ethan Callahan and his brothers were remote-control hogs. Come to think about it, they weren't the only ones.

Though, if he could give a friendly nudge here and there with Cheyenne and Emily, he'd gladly give up the remote.

Eden came out of the kitchen wearing an apron, her red hair caught back off her face with glittery butterfly clips that matched the blue of her sweater.

She smiled at Emily. "Good, your arms are empty. Take advantage of it and come keep me company in the kitchen. The men are in charge of the kids today."

Opal raised a brow, Alicia tucked easily in the crook of her arm. "Girl, you're asking for trouble there. Sister and I'll just keep an eye on the toms, make sure they don't get to strutting and forget their business."

Eden grinned. "That's fine, then, Opal. When you feel like being a hen, just come on in."

Emily followed Eden into the spacious kitchen with its granite countertops, tile floors and state-of-the-art appliances. It was a chef's dream. And Eden was in her element, stirring this and adding a pinch of that and making it all look so easy.

"I heard one of your business associates came out. We'd have been happy to have him join us."

"He had to get back to Washington." Emily sat down at the table because Eden's constant movement was making her tired, and she was still only averaging three hours of sleep a night, if that. "Did the whole town know I had a visitor?"

Eden glanced over her shoulder. "Of course. Think of where he stayed."

At the boardinghouse. "Oh. Right. I don't think Cheyenne liked him."

Eden peeled potatoes and added them to a huge pot on the stove. "Why not?"

"I don't know. He was sort of...territorial, if you know what I mean."

"Mmm. He was being a male."

Emily had to laugh. "Yes, I guess. Seemed silly considering our circumstances." That was another thing that most everyone knew—that she and Cheyenne were only married for the sake of propriety and the children. "Can I do anything to help?"

"Just keep me company. I work better alone. Do me a favor, though. When Dora shows up, head her off or hide the potato peeler. I love her to death, but she's a menace in the kitchen."

"I'm afraid I'm not much better, but I can certainly set the table or dish olives out of a jar."

"Stony took care of that before ya'll got here. Nikki," she said without turning around, "don't even think about giving Rosie that candy bar."

Rosie was a black setter who followed the little girl around like a shadow.

"But he's havin' a regular chocolate fit."

A male dog with a female name. Cute. And Nikki, Emily noticed, had adopted Eden's Southern accent. Even cuter.

"I'm sure he'll survive."

Nikki flipped up the dog's ear and whispered something, then hurried out of the room.

"That doesn't bode well," Eden said, amusement and love tingeing her voice.

"Do you want me to check on her?"

"I imagine Stony'll keep an eye out. The man's got an uncanny knack for knowing what's going on." Her voice went all dreamy and Emily felt a crazy jolt of envy.

She watched the efficient way Eden worked and talked and seemed to take everything in stride. The woman had a four-month-old baby, as well as the six-year-old, and she was cooking a feast for more than twenty people.

Debbie would have been just like this. Domestic. In her element. The wave of sadness stung her throat and eyes.

"Doesn't all this make you nervous?" she asked.

"Entertaining? No. I'm a caterer by trade. I've fed five hundred at a sitting."

"Better you than me. When do you sleep?"

"Ah, the twins are still keeping you up nights, hmm? It'll even out soon. Sarah's sleeping through the night now, bless her darlin' little heart. Though Stony's not. He gets up just to check on her. Cryin' out loud, the man'd wake her up if I let him. He dotes on those girls."

They'd named their baby girl after Stony's deaf grandmother, the woman who'd raised the gentle giant of a cowboy, taught him to speak with a touch and listen with his heart. Emily thought it was a beautiful tribute to the woman.

Just as she had named Hunter and Alicia as a tribute to their parents—Debbie and Jimmy.

"Well, I've got everything under control in here. What do you say we wander in and see how badly our babies are being spoiled? If they're not being taught any bad habits, we'll find ourselves a soft couch and put our feet up.'' She turned, paused. ''Oh, something's got you sad.''

Emily shook her head. ''My sister was a lot like you. Always cooking or gardening, taking care of the neighbors' kids and the ones at the preschool where she worked. I hate it that she missed seeing the twins. I feel like a worn-out dishrag, and I'm certain she'd have been fresh as a daisy.''

''You're missing her. That's natural.'' Eden slipped an arm through Emily's as they left the kitchen. ''I've never lost anyone close to me, so I can't begin to imagine your heartache. If you'll let us, though, we'll try to ease it.''

Emily, battling her emotions, managed to whisper, ''Thank you. It's good to be here.''

Cheyenne looked up as she came into the room, his brows dipping. He moved to her side and that odd, inexplicable connection they'd always shared seemed even stronger.

He slid a hand under her hair, cupped the back of her neck, held her against his side. ''Holidays are the roughest.''

She nodded, hardly surprised he knew her thoughts. ''Debbie loved Thanksgiving. We were raised on bread stuffing cooked in the bird, but Jimmy craved cornbread dressing. She made both. The look on his face when he realized she'd gone to that extra trouble for him is still etched in my mind. I swear he fell in love with her all over again. They were lucky to have each other.''

"Yes." He pressed a soft kiss to her temple. "And we're lucky to have their children."

She let him hold her for a moment longer, because it simply felt too good, then at last pulled back. She didn't want to give their friends the wrong impression about their relationship.

Everyone knew they'd married for the sake of the babies. And after the grapevine had chewed thoroughly on Dave Kimble's quick visit, they were surely reminded that she had a job to return to before long.

As the house filled with neighbors and happy children and babies, Emily began to relax. She couldn't help but get caught up in the festive mood.

Pastor Dan Lucas showed up, his booming laughter preceding him into the house. You always knew where the man was in the room by his laugh. It made her smile. The cigar in his pocket raised her brow.

Chance Hammond came in behind him, spotted Emily and Cheyenne and moved in their direction.

"Finally ventured out with the babies?"

Emily smiled sheepishly. "Does everyone in this town know I'm scared to death to take the kids out by myself?"

"Probably not everyone, but close." He grinned. "How you doing?"

"Good."

"She's tired," Cheyenne said as though the doctor should fix that problem immediately.

Chance grinned. "Comes with the territory."

"Where are Kelly and the girls?" Emily asked, looking around. She'd formed a bond with Chance's assistant, who'd graciously stopped by the ranch several times to check on her and the babies. She hadn't known Kelly had children of her own and had been especially touched by Kelly's youngest daughter, Kimberly, a beautiful cherub who spoke eloquently with her wide, round eyes, yet never uttered a word. Emily imagined there was heartache associated with that silence, but she hadn't wanted to pry.

"Claimed she was coming down with a bug."

Hmm, Emily thought. If she hadn't been looking closely, she would have missed the subtle tightening of the skin at the corners of his mouth.

"Seems it'd be right up your alley to substantiate that claim, you being a doctor and all," Cheyenne commented. Evidently he, too, had noticed the undercurrents his friend didn't know he projected.

"She wouldn't sit still for it. Didn't want to take a chance of passing any phantom germs to any of the babies."

"You'll take her and those sweet girls a plate of food, then," Iris Brewer said, overhearing their conversation.

"Yes, ma'am, I imagine I could do that."

Emily hid a smile. It appeared that Iris was subtly joining forces with her husband and his pals and trying her hand at a little nudging.

Emily hadn't cared for such meddling when she'd been a kid who found herself in hot water more times than not. Cheyenne's nickname for her, trouble, had certainly been apt.

But she didn't seem as jinxed now, and the meddling didn't seem quite so invasive.

As long as she wasn't on the receiving end of it, that is.

Just then, one of the babies started crying.

Mortified, Emily felt her milk begin to flow—right through her bra and onto the front of her sweater.

She saw Cheyenne's gaze shift to her breasts, looked at him with wide eyes she knew were panicked.

She'd spoken—or thought—too soon.

"It's this town," she whispered. "I'm forever doomed to embarrassment."

"No need for embarrassment. If you'll look around, there are two other women in this room with wet shirts."

She did look. Both Eden and Dora were plucking at their sweater fronts. With his law-enforcement training, Cheyenne was a man who noticed details. The rest of the group was looking around to see which one of the babies was crying.

"Sorry about that, girls," Dora said with a laugh, picking up Ryan, who'd started the fussing. Now the other infants were joining in. "All it takes is one baby to cry, and every nursing mother in town needs a blouse change."

Emily sighed, looked at Cheyenne. "Boy or girl?"

"Boy. I fed Alicia last time."

EMILY KNEW SHE NEEDED to get out with the babies on her own. They were a month old, for heaven's sake.

Thanksgiving had been sort of a trial run, but she'd had Cheyenne there to help.

It was past time to show a little backbone.

"Okay, my pretty girl and handsome boy. We're going on an outing today. Just a quick visit to Tillis' General Store. We've got to do this on our own sometime, and it might as well be today."

She tied a pink cap on Alicia's head and a blue one on Hunter's. They were so darn cute she felt her confidence growing.

"The sun is shining and the snow's not falling yet and you're both running out of diapers. It'll be fun. You'll see. And you'll both be angels and not make me look bad, won't you."

The diaper bag was already packed with enough stuff to last a weekend trip, rather than the mere hour she expected to be gone. Still, she wanted to be prepared.

Now the trick was to get it all out to the car.

She took a breath, looked around, refusing to acknowledge that her insides were trembling and it would take very little to talk her out of the whole exercise.

The babies were strapped into their infant seats, both resting in the middle of the big kitchen table.

"Okay, stay right there, you two. I'll be back in a flash." With the diaper bag clutched in her hand, she dashed out the back door.

Cold December air burned her nose and bit her cheeks. The blinding glare of sun in a clear blue sky made her eyes water. She tossed the diaper bag into the trunk on top of the stroller, opened all the car doors and sprinted back into the house.

It only took her a minute or less, but she felt guilty for leaving the kids in the house by themselves. Were there laws against this? How did one person accomplish this by herself? she wondered, sweating.

She started to strip off her coat, then realized that would only be one more thing to carry, so she left it on.

"Okay, let's get organized." She laid out her purse and slipped her car keys in her pocket. Should she try carrying both infant seats at once, or one at a time?

She lifted one of the seats by its attached handle, then the other, testing their weight. It was a cumbersome burden, but not unmanageable.

Before she could take a step or figure out how to pick up her purse now that her hands were full and straining with babies, Alicia started to cry.

"Oh, sweetie, what's the matter?" She set both seats back on the table and slipped her hand beneath Alicia.

"Who wet your pants?" she asked rhetorically as Alicia poked out her little lip and whimpered. "Okay, okay, shush. We'll fix it." At this rate it would be dinnertime before they made it out of the house.

She sighed, lifted Alicia out of the seat and laid her on the table with a blanket beneath. She had the tapes undone and the diaper wadded up before she realized she hadn't gotten out a clean one. Worse yet, the last of the supply was packed in the diaper bag—in the trunk of the car.

Great. Wrapping the baby back in the blanket—her little bottom still naked—she put her in the infant seat, fastened the strap and dashed back out to the car. Snagging a diaper from the trunk, she raced back in, imagining that she looked like a lunatic running a one-woman relay race. Thank goodness no one was watching.

"Round two, second verse." She was panting, and now she did remove her jacket. Once again she unwrapped the baby and set about to accomplish the diaper change. She was a wreck and her hands were shaking, and she hadn't even started the car.

"Hunter, if you have to go to the bathroom, please do so before we get on the road." She nearly laughed at herself. She'd heard her mother say those same words to her and Debbie countless times. They'd moved several times and spent a lot of time on the road traveling. Tamara hated using dirty gas-station rest rooms or a bush by the side of the road when that was the only option. Considered it terribly uncivilized, so she always made sure everyone started a journey with an empty bladder.

She'd just fastened the tapes and stuffed Alicia's legs back into the pink corduroy jumper when someone knocked on the open kitchen door.

Emily jumped and whirled around.

Cheyenne's uncle stood in the open doorway, silent and watchful. It was a look she'd seen on Cheyenne's face countless times.

"I am John White Cloud."

"Yes, I know." She'd seen him several times over

the last month at the ranch, but he'd never come in to meet her. And since she was usually occupied with the kids, she hadn't had the opportunity to go out and introduce herself. She'd asked Cheyenne about it, and he'd simply said there was no second-guessing his uncle. The man had his own agenda, claimed he would come soon bearing gifts.

Well, if he'd already bought the gifts, they'd likely not fit by now. The babies were growing right before her eyes.

"Would you like to come in and see your greatniece and -nephew?"

The tall, gray-haired man stared at her, then stepped silently into the room and gazed down at the babies. She wondered if he'd witnessed her mad dashes between the car and the house. Probably.

He looked up at her, his brown eyes giving away none of his thoughts, his weathered skin sporting squint lines that fanned toward his temples. "You are going on a journey?"

She frowned. Oh, he thought she was leaving. "No. Just to the store. The babies are out of diapers."

He frowned. "You do not wash them?"

Wash them? "Oh, they're not that type. I'm using disposable."

He shook his head, clearly puzzled. "Young people throw their money away on unnecessary expenses."

"Not really. With me, it's more a case of selfpreservation. I'm a bit of a novice at all this—but you probably already figured that out if you saw me running around like a chicken without its head."

Her attempt to lighten his mood fell flat.

"You would do well to use the stroller that is folded in your trunk. It will hold both children and all of their needs. Then you need only to roll it outdoors and make one trip."

"I didn't think of that."

He studied her in a way she found most unnerving.

"I will be happy to go to the store for you."

She was tempted to take him up on the offer. It was twelve degrees out and she was sweating like a hog. Her nerves were already shot, and she hadn't even started the car. But she'd been cooped up in the house for a month. Most new mothers would be traipsing through the mall after a couple of days. She had to face this, get it out of the way.

And then there was pride. She didn't want John White Cloud thinking she was a complete ninny.

"Thank you for the offer, but I've got to take the plunge sometime. I haven't taken the babies out by myself yet, so this is sort of like a field trip for me and the kids—though I don't know how others do it. I don't seem to have enough hands for everything."

He nodded ever so slightly. "I will lend you mine, then, to help you get started on your…field trip." A ghost of a smile played at his lips and flirted with his serious brown eyes.

Well, Emily thought. A reaction.

Having spoken his intention, he lifted Hunter's infant seat and scooped up her purse, leaving her to follow with Alicia. She trailed behind him and waited while he strapped both children into the back seat of the car. He made it look so darned easy.

He straightened and gave her another of those long looks. "You are troubled?"

"If you want to know the truth, it's a bit demoralizing for me not to be in control of something as simple as loading children into the car."

He laid a hand on her shoulder. "You did not plan for this fork in the road of your life. It is a good thing you have done for my fair nephew. There are not many women with your heart and bravery."

Why did people keep insisting she was some sort of heroine? "It's nothing, really."

His eyes were soft as they rested on her. "I think I will like you, Emily Vincent Bodine."

She smiled then, somehow knowing she'd passed a test, that his words were indeed high praise. "And I, you, John White Cloud. Thank you for the help."

"You're welcome. And you will drive safely in this flashy car of yours."

She laughed. Just like a man to look longingly at a vehicle. She vowed to figure out a way to let him drive the Mercedes before she left Montana.

The twins fell asleep on the way to town and Emily was gaining confidence with each mile. This wasn't so hard, after all. So what if she'd had a little help getting everything into the car? It would have been foolish and rude to refuse John White Cloud's help. And futile, she thought, since he'd given her little choice in the matter.

That must be where Cheyenne had inherited his bossy, steamroller tendencies.

When she pulled up in front of Tillis' General Store, she gave herself a moment to think things through. She wouldn't be able to get both kids in the shopping cart—there wouldn't be room for the groceries. She could always put them in their own carts and push both, but that seemed silly. So she took John's advice and loaded everything into the stroller.

Feeling like a can-do girl, shoulders back, head held high, she went into the store as if she knew her business.

Pulling the stroller with one hand, she pushed the cart with the other...right into a neatly stacked display of canned peas.

As she wasn't watching, she wasn't prepared for the disaster. The crashing cans scared her to death and startled the kids into crying.

She went hot and then cold. Tiny cylinders rolled every which way and she dived after them. Thank goodness nothing was breakable.

Emily had heard of Murphy's Law where everything went wrong. In her case, it seemed to be Shotgun Ridge Law.

She was mortified.

Even more so when she heard a familiar chuckle behind her.

Oh, she simply wanted to die.

She looked up, glared. "If you say one word, Bodine, I swear you'll be eating that hat."

He held up his hands in a gesture of surrender,

though his handsome face was creased in a grin. He maneuvered the stroller out of the fray and handed it off to Vera, who had come running when the peas had tumbled. Good grief, she didn't need any more witnesses to her clumsiness.

"What are you doing here?" Emily snatched at a slippery can and broke a fingernail. "Are you following me?"

He didn't speak, just stood there, his brown eyes dancing with amusement, hat tipped back on his head, looking sexier than any man had a right to. His uniform shirt was tucked into a pair of jeans that hugged his hips in a way that surely ought to be considered indecent for a public servant—in her opinion.

And why was she dwelling on the man's anatomy? She was in the middle of a mortifying personal crisis.

"Well?" she demanded, fielding another can of peas.

"Am I allowed to speak?"

She rolled her eyes. "Yes."

"Good. I just had lunch and I don't think I have room to eat my hat." He squatted down next to her. "Need a hand there, trouble?"

Before she thought better of it, she reached out and gave him a poke. He was off balance enough to go sprawling on his behind.

She blinked, horrified, opened her mouth to apologize. He stunned her by laughing out loud, long and hard.

"Idiot," she muttered, and felt her own amusement tickle her insides, twitch at her lips.

Here they sat, right there in the middle of the floor with cans of peas scattered all around them and customers peeking around the aisles, and the man was laughing like a loon. He should have had the good sense to be embarrassed.

Yet did he act like she'd expected? No.

And why couldn't the place have been deserted?

"Jinxed," she said. "I'm sure of it."

Vera started to come to their aid, having passed the now quieted twins off to a couple of customers to cuddle and coo at, but Cheyenne waved her off. Thank goodness. Emily didn't know if she could handle being any more mortified.

"What is it with me and this town? Put us together, and the planets align to rain down disaster. Tongues will be wagging. They'll say, 'There goes that Vincent girl—'"

"Bodine," he corrected.

"Even worse. 'There goes the sheriff's lady, mowing down canned goods and gathering speeding tickets, and Lord knows what she'll do next.'" Emily hugged an aluminum can to her chest. "I'm a mess."

He reached out and touched her cheek in that gentle way of his. "You're beautiful."

She drew in a breath. Her hair was frizzed from the cold, she'd yet to lose the weight she'd put on during pregnancy, she'd knocked down an entire display of canned peas, and the man just touched her softly and told her she was beautiful.

And then he did something she was totally unprepared for. He leaned forward and pressed his lips to hers. In front of God and everybody in Tillis' General Store, he kissed her until her soul sang, kissed her with gentleness and reverence and a single-minded purpose that made her want to weep.

He drew back slowly, held her with his velvety brown eyes. "There," he whispered. "A kiss to make it better."

Her heart squeezed, then pounded like an ink press on high speed.

Oh, no. It couldn't be happening. Not now. Not this.

But it was.

It hit her with the force of a body blow to her heart. Six simple words. *A kiss to make it better.*

And Emily tumbled headlong in love with Cheyenne Bodine.

In love with her own husband.

Chapter Eleven

With eyes blurry from sleep, Emily glanced at the clock on the table beside the bed. She'd hardly gotten any rest between the twins and her own thoughts keeping her awake, and it was time to get up.

Now that she'd admitted she was in love with Cheyenne, she couldn't think of anything else. It colored her every move, her every breath. Scared her to death.

Why had she never realized so many things scared her? Here she'd thought she was a tough-as-nails businesswoman, yet life was pelting her with one uncertain missile after another. And she kept finding herself cowering, instead of dodging.

And thinking. Probing deeper and deeper, seeking answers for a life that seemed to be on a runaway train.

She'd chosen to spend her maternity leave in Shotgun Ridge, seeking a place where someone would care. Oh, she could have *paid* someone to care, but she'd desperately wanted it to come from the heart. She'd lost her sister, and her own mother couldn't be bothered to stick around and hold her hand.

She admitted now that a kernel of longing, a fleeting fantasy that she hadn't been able to shove back quick enough, had sneaked into her subconscious.

And that yearning and fantasy had to do with Cheyenne Bodine.

She hadn't known she'd carried a torch for him in her young heart, a flame that had smoldered and fired into adulthood. She wouldn't have guessed it was there, had been too busy building a life and a career to let it surface, to examine it.

Well, she was examining it now. It was all she could think of.

The real question was, had she come back to Shotgun Ridge for the children or for herself?

Had some part of her she'd never acknowledged wanted to see if there was something between Cheyenne and her now that they were grown? Had love always been there, waiting to be set free? Sure, she'd felt giddy at the thought of seeing him again, but she'd never allowed herself to probe more deeply, to admit that something more lurked.

And there was definitely more. On her part at least.

But how would their worlds ever mesh?

It was a question she couldn't answer.

But the here and now, well, that was a different matter. Each time he glanced her way, her heart would lurch and she wondered if he could see the emotion written on her face, in her body movements.

She'd embarrassed herself half to death in town two days ago, yet he found her situation sweet, tried to make her feel better by admitting that he'd once knocked down a whole shelf of dill pickles in Vera's store. And that had been a hell of a mess to clean up, he'd said.

Well, like falling off a horse, she knew she had to get back on. So she planned to go into town again today. Show her face and see if she turned to stone or something.

And because she had an agenda, she needed to start early. Otherwise the kids would be awake and she'd never get dressed.

Stumbling into the bathroom, still half-asleep, she turned on the tub's hot-water tap and started to peel her nightgown over her head. Movement caught her eye.

She gave a tiny shriek, caught the arrested, astonished look on Cheyenne's face, and yanked the gown back to her knees. "Good grief!"

With razor in midswipe, his eyes were glued to the reflection of her he could obviously see in the mirror.

A white towel was wrapped around his lean waist.

And that was all he wore.

Just a towel.

A small towel. Small enough that, a tiny little tug and it would fall to the floor.

Small enough that she could clearly see the effect desire had on the male anatomy as he automatically turned halfway toward her.

Oh, dear, sweet heaven, the man made her mouth water.

Her gaze finally lifted to his.

Wiping shaving cream off his face, he turned the

rest of the way around. Brave man, she thought, not the least concerned about his arousal.

"Um...I didn't see you there."

"I figured that out between 'eek' and 'good grief.' Come here."

"What?"

"Come here."

Her heart lurched right into her throat, pounded. She took a step, was helpless to do anything less.

He met her halfway. His hands slid under her hair. His body was warm, his bare chest pressing against her breasts.

"If we don't do this, neither one of us is going to be worth a damn."

And with that, he lowered his mouth to hers.

She closed her eyes, gave in, melted against him. Through the thin material of the towel she could feel his desire. Could he feel hers?

His palm pressed against her back, nestling her against his arousal, setting her on fire. She wanted to climb right up his body, inside his body.

His tongue explored her mouth as his hands angled her head for better access. He molded her to his will and she let him.

Oh, she let him...and she helped him. She wrapped her arms around his neck, rose on tiptoe, poured herself into the kiss, drinking from him, taking everything he offered.

She couldn't breathe, didn't understand it. Steam rose around them from the running bathwater.

He eased her out of the kiss when she didn't have the strength to do it herself.

Her brain was as foggy as the steamy air of the bathroom.

"What...what brought that on?"

"We've been dancing around it for days, maybe even years. Ever since the avalanche of peas, you've been looking at me with a hunger that's damned hard to resist."

"I haven't."

He smiled. "Liar."

She took a deep breath to steady herself. "You're a potent man, Bodine."

"Likewise, Bodine. And because of that, I'm walking out of this room before I lose my mind completely and do something neither of us is ready for."

"Speak for yourself." Oh, Lord. She hadn't meant to blurt that out.

He groaned, stepped back and shook his head. "You forget I was in that delivery room with you."

The reminder had her frowning. She felt pretty good. Felt healed. And when Cheyenne took her in his arms, the memory of giving birth to babies was the furthest thing from her mind.

There was no denying the sexual tension building in the household. All it took was their being in the same room, and sparks crackled like hot electrical wires without a ground. They were arcing off each other's emotions.

And it was becoming nearly impossible to keep a lid on those emotions.

He ran a finger down her nose. "The bathroom's all yours, trouble."

Mmm-hmm. And her agenda for the day had just changed. Perhaps she was making a mistake. Most likely a big one.

But the want inside her was bigger than any she'd ever known.

At least once before she left, she wanted to know her husband in every sense of the word.

They were two adults. They could handle a mature relationship. If she was going to leave Shotgun Ridge carrying love in her heart, she wanted to carry something more, too.

She wanted to carry the memory of Cheyenne Bodine's touch, the feel of him inside her.

EMILY PARKED in front of the Bagley widows' boardinghouse and didn't have to worry about the baby shuffle. The ladies came right outside as though they'd been watching for her.

She glanced across the street at the sheriff's station, but didn't see Cheyenne's beefy Bronco parked in its usual spot.

The widows moved down the porch steps—raced, rather, Emily noted—all but shoving each other to see who would get to the car first. Emily bit the inside of her cheek.

"What a wonderful surprise!" Opal said. "Are you here for a visit or meeting that husband of yours?"

"Don't be dense, Opal. The girl's got eyes in her head and knows when her own husband's truck's not in sight." Mildred leaned down to peek in the car window at the twins, wiggling her fingers as though fully expecting the babies to wave back. "Saw him drive off not twenty minutes ago. You commented on it yourself when you were spying out the window."

"*You* were the one spying. And how do you know he won't be right back, expecting to meet his wife?"

Emily decided she ought to speak and put an end to the bickering before it turned into a brawl. It would be a shame for the widows to have to move their residence across the street—to the jailhouse. Not that Cheyenne would lock them up. Now that young deputy, Boyd, she recalled, might. If he'd write a pregnant woman a speeding ticket, he might well arrest two little old ladies.

"Actually," she said, "I was wondering if the baby-sitting offer still stood. I know I should have called first, but—"

"Of *course* we'll sit! We're minding Kelly Anderson's sweet little girls, as well, and they'll be delighted. That little one, Kimberly, with her voice trapped inside her that way just tears your heart out. Maybe the babies'll get a peep out of her. Sister, run around and get Hunter. I'll get Alicia." Opal had the car door open before Emily could shut her mouth. "Oh, we're thrilled. Just thrilled."

Emily might as well have not been standing there, for all the notice the widows paid her. They were too busy unbuckling car seats, plucking babies, cooing and clucking and smiling. She probably could have taken a walk around the block and they'd never even know she'd been gone.

Grinning, she grabbed the diaper bag and followed them onto the wide front porch and into the white clapboard house.

The boardinghouse smelled liked every child's memory—apples, cinnamon, spices and evergreen.

Christmas scents.

A Douglas fir stood in the corner of the living room, decorated like a grand Victorian lady with lace and angels, tinsel and brightly colored balls, the fragrant branches twinkling with miniature white lights.

Although Christmas was more than three weeks away, there were gaily wrapped packages beneath the tree, resting on cotton batting artfully arranged to resemble snow.

"Would you like some hot cider, dear? We've a pot of it on the stove."

"Thank you, but I don't really have the time. I've booked an appointment over at Arletta's beauty shop, and I'm due in a few minutes. I'd have taken the twins with me, but I worried that the chemical smells might be too much for them."

Mildred perked up at the mention of the beauty shop. "What a splendid idea. Not asphyxiating the babies with permanent-wave solution," she clarified, "but taking the time to pamper yourself. What are you having done?"

"Just a trim, and maybe have my highlights refreshed."

"Well, Arletta's your woman. Had her put a few of

those streaks in my own hair.'' Holding Hunter in one arm, Mildred passed a hand over her pageboy.

"It looks very nice."

Opal snorted. "She's an old woman with a mile-wide streak of vanity. You young girls look fabulous in the latest styles. Some people I'll not mention ought to act their age."

Mildred cocked a brow. "Just because you're gray as a mule and have shorn your hair for practicality is no reason to cast stones at those of us who have a care…and a sex drive."

Opal gasped. "Mind the children's ears!"

Mildred smirked.

Emily wanted to stay and see how this conversation played out—especially the part about the sex drive—but she was late. And she had an idea the banter was really just for her benefit.

"Um," she ventured, "I should be going if you're sure you don't mind watching the kids."

"Of course we don't. Stay as long as you want."

"I should only be a couple of hours. I've scheduled an appointment with Dr. Hammond at one o'clock."

"Is he seeing the children, as well?" Opal asked.

"Yes."

"Well, then, leave us your carriage and we'll push the little ones over to meet you. No sense loading them in the car when the office is just around the corner. Little Jessica and Kimberly Anderson are upstairs dressing right now, but I'm sure they'll love a chance to get some fresh air and pay a quick visit to their momma, who, of course you know, works over at the clinic with Chance.''

''Yes, I know. Are you sure, though, about keeping the twins that long? I mean, there're enough bottles and diapers to last, but I hate to impose.''

''Impose, ha!'' Mildred said. ''The second you walk out the door, Sister'll call everyone to brag about getting to baby-sit, and you can bet they'll all come running. We'll have a regular bevy of grandmas here doting on the children. Off with you now. And don't worry about a thing.''

Emily fussed over the babies and listed everything she could think of that the widows might need to know. She was wondering aloud if she should write out an emergency medical note when the ladies practically pushed her out the door.

Leaving the stroller as instructed, she drove down the street and around the corner to the beauty shop. It felt odd to be all alone. She kept thinking she was forgetting something.

And though she had complete trust in Mildred and Opal, it made her heart squeeze to leave the babies, made her feel precariously close to tears. What in the world would she do when she had to drop them off at day care when she went back to work?

She pushed through the door of the beauty salon, and a wreath with silly blinking eyes belted out a tinny Christmas tune. Astonished, startled, she grinned. Here, too, the interior was festooned with holiday decorations. She'd have to get Cheyenne to bring home a tree before all the good ones were picked over and bought up.

Arletta, in her late forties, wearing tight blue jeans, cowboy boots and a man's shirt that hung to mid-thigh, waved her in and patted the swivel chair in front of her station.

"Come in, come in. You're right on time. But where are those babies?"

"I left them with Mildred and Opal Bagley." Should she call and check on them? Her cell phone was in her purse. A lot could happen in five minutes. One of them could choke or—

"Mmm. Corrupt them early."

Emily's eyes snapped to Arletta's in the mirror.

Arletta laughed. "Just kidding, hon. Those ladies are harmless. And the best sitters in town. Your babies will be fine."

Emily knew that. She didn't know why she'd had such a reaction. Such a *motherly* reaction.

"So, what are we doing today?" Arletta ran her hands through Emily's thick hair.

Emily took a breath, ordered herself to relax and enjoy her time out. "Highlights and a trim. I got a good look at myself the other day and realized I looked like a hag. I've hardly had a second to myself. I'm starting to feel like a giant walking baby bottle, and I decided I needed to treat myself to a little pampering."

Arletta laughed. "That's the spirit. And you've come to the right place. Your beautician use bleach or color?"

"Bleach, I think."

"Then we'll just get started. That's Miz Pearson over there under the first dryer." An older woman with pink perm rods wound in her hair leaned forward and waved. "Louanne Tucker is over there primping in my makeup, and that's Miz Pearson's daughter reading *Vogue* magazine."

Emily smiled and nodded and Arletta got to work, chatting easily. In no time at all Emily's hair was sectioned with alternate strands, painted with bleach solution and wrapped in tinfoil.

"You caught me at the right time, as I've got a bit of a lull. Town's getting so populated I'm having trouble keeping up with business. Gonna have to hire an assistant soon." Arletta folded the last foil and glanced down at Emily's hands. "Nails a little weak since we took off the acrylics?"

Emily curled her fingers inward. "They look pretty sad, don't they?"

"We'll fix that right up. Come on over to the nail station and I'll give you a manicure and pedicure—on the house. Since you didn't have a baby shower, this'll be my gift."

Emily couldn't imagine her own manicurist in Seattle offering free services.

While Emily's feet soaked in a bucket of warm soapy water and her hands rested on the manicure table, Arletta and the other women imparted gossip, made girl talk and shamelessly pried information from Emily about her life in Washington and her job. Emily couldn't resist running some of the ad campaigns by them. She had her own little focus group here and might as well test the market. The happy face was unanimously voted in, and Emily realized she was simply going to have to get over her bias.

Her bare foot was propped on Arletta's knee for the promised pedicure when she looked out the window and glimpsed a familiar truck passing by.

Cheyenne.

Her heart thumped, and Arletta must have felt the pulse, because she looked, too.

The Bronco cruised slowly down the street, raised high off the ground on its huge knobby tires, bars of emergency lights on top. She saw Blue sitting beside Cheyenne on the front seat, eyes alert as though he had a star pinned to his furry coat and was taking his patrol duty very seriously.

She knew the instant Cheyenne spotted her car, saw him slow and scan the storefront. Oh, Lord, she hoped he couldn't see through the salon's windows. She scrunched down in the chair and Arletta's file slipped and plowed across the top of her toes.

She had tinfoil sticking out of her head like an alien from another planet. It was scary enough to frighten a Martian half to death. She did *not* want Cheyenne to see her looking like this.

"Hmm," Arletta hummed as she buffed and filed Emily's toenails. "How old did you say those babies are now?"

"Five weeks."

The woman smiled. "Rekindled the romance with my Earl after four weeks. I imagine if I was married to the likes of Cheyenne Bodine, I wouldn't have waited that long.''

Emily's face heated. Was she that obvious? Did everyone in the beauty shop see her sexual desire for her husband?

IT WAS ONLY FIVE-THIRTY, but it was dark outside and the kids were already in their crib asleep. She'd brought home takeout from Brewer's and wondered if she should heat it up. Cheyenne hadn't come in from the barn yet. She was fairly glowing with pride that she'd unloaded both babies by herself and gotten them settled without having to shout for help.

Changes were afoot.

She looked out the kitchen window, wondering what was keeping Cheyenne. Light spilled out of the barn and a nearly full moon shone over ground upholstered in packed snow.

Christmas lights blinked on, strands of colorful bulbs strung all along the eaves of the barn and outlining the double doors. ''Oh,'' she breathed.

She reached for her coat, draped it across her shoulders and stepped out onto the porch. Cheyenne was sitting on the wicker bench, obviously admiring his handiwork.

''It's beautiful,'' she said.

He glanced up at her. ''I need to reset the timer so they'll come on earlier.''

She sat beside him on the bench, enjoying the night and the mood. The air was cold, but that only added to the festive air. What was it about simple strands of glass balls shimmering with color that could make the stomach flutter and the heart fill?

The season for miracles. A time of anticipation and hope. Oh, she loved it all.

"I can't wait for the babies to see this."

He glanced over at her and smiled. "They in bed?"

"Yes."

"Your hair looks nice."

"Thank you. Did you notice it?"

"That's what I just said, didn't I?"

"No, I meant, did you notice I had it done by looking at it or because you saw me at the beauty shop?"

His lips twitched. "I wasn't following you, if that's what you're getting at. Your car was out front."

"But could you see through the windows?" She'd meant this to come out as a casual question. Instead, it sounded like a demand.

He reached over and gathered a lock of her hair, bringing it to his nose, inhaling the scent. "'Course not. Arletta's got her name scrawled across the tinted glass. Makes it darn near impossible to see if a lady's getting her fingernails worked on or has tinfoil antennas sticking out of her head."

She smacked him.

"Hey, what was that for?"

"A woman wants a man to appreciate the final glamour, not the process."

He fisted his hand in her hair for an instant, his gaze steady on hers. "I'm appreciating the glamour. A little too much."

"Oh." She'd been worried about him seeing her

looking like a Martian and had made it sound as if she was looking for approval. "I wasn't fishing for compliments."

"I know. That's why I like to give them." He sniffed her hair again, combed his fingers through the length. "You don't consider yourself extraordinary when you are. You don't play off your looks when you could easily do so."

"Oh, no, I can't."

"Yes, you can. But you don't. That's why it's such a pleasure to give you compliments. Honest ones." He let go of her hair and leaned back on the bench, enjoying the night and the way the colored lights on the barn glittered across the snow.

"I was engaged once to a very beautiful woman." He wasn't sure why that popped out.

"You were?"

She sounded so surprised. He didn't take offense. "For all of two days. Her name was Linda. And she *did* need compliments. Thrived on them. But they were never enough. She flaunted and flounced and used her looks to every advantage."

"What happened?"

"She decided city life was more her speed. Couldn't see tying herself to a small-town sheriff on a modest mustang ranch."

"Then why in the world did she accept your proposal?"

He raised a brow. "Passion can make a person say things they regret in the light of day."

"Oh."

He glanced at her, knew he didn't need to supply details.

She reached for his hand, surprising him. They sat quietly for a moment, listening to the horses shifting and murmuring to each other, watching the shadows of the moon and Christmas lights casting colorful rainbows in the snow.

"I'm sorry she hurt you," she said softly, her breath puffing in the cold air.

Cheyenne shrugged. "It was for the best. Better to find out before the wedding."

"Well, if you don't mind me saying so, she sounds perfectly awful."

He felt a grin tug. "I don't mind. Did you take the kids to the beauty shop with you?"

"No, Mildred and Opal watched them. I'm surprised you didn't know that. I'm told there was a crowd of grandmotherly types at the boardinghouse."

"I didn't make it back to the station until after two."

"Oh, I was already at the doctor's office by then."

His heart somersaulted. "Everything okay?"

"Perfect. The babies have each grown an inch and gained two pounds."

"And you?"

The words hung in the cold night air as she looked at him. Steadily. With a hint of challenge. "One hundred percent back in commission."

He leaned forward, elbows on his knees and tugged at his hat. "I wish you hadn't told me that."

"Why?"

"Because it's going to keep me awake."

"Seems a shame to stay awake thinking about something when you could be doing something about it."

He swore and came up off of the bench like a shot. "Damn it, trouble. We're not going down that road."

"Then what was that kiss about in the bathroom this morning?"

"Hormones."

"Well, if you want to talk about hormones, I've become somewhat of an expert on them lately."

He glared at her. "What's gotten into you?"

"You."

His hands fisted at his side as though that would keep him from reaching for her. She knew he wanted her. And darn it all, her hair was fixed, her nails done, toes painted and she'd shaved her legs. The babies were sleeping like lambs.

She stood and went to him, raising a brow when he took a step back. She didn't have a whole lot of experience seducing a man, but this one was worth it.

"Will you answer a simple question?"

"You rarely ask simple questions, trouble."

"Do you want to make love with me?"

His chest rose and fell, his breath puffing out in front of him in a white cloud of vapor. "This wasn't part of the bargain."

"Bargains change."

"Is that what you want?"

"More than I ever thought I could."

He looked into her eyes, took her in with his steady

gaze, his utterly complete focus. She saw the beginning of surrender. His fingertips were cold against her cheek, featherlight, unsteady.

The brim of his hat brushed her head as he leaned down, his breath warm against her lips. And still he watched her, studied her as though she was the only gift under the tree and he was afraid to tug on the ribbon, to unwrap his wish.

"Do you know what you do to me?"

She shook her head, could do nothing more. His touch was like fire against her skin.

"I think this has been coming since we were kids."

A long time. She'd thought the same. "Then kiss me. Make love with me."

"Damn near everything inside me's saying no."

Close. His lips were so close. Her heart hammered and her hands clutched at his jacket. "And the damn near part?" she whispered. "What's it saying?"

He reached behind her, pushed open the door and walked her backward into the kitchen. "It's saying hallelujah."

Chapter Twelve

He shut the door behind them, stripped off his coat and hers and at last indulged in the kiss he was aching for. Her warm skin smelled of vanilla. The faint scent of salon chemicals clung to her hair.

He threaded his fingers through the thick strands, cupped her head, held her just there so he could enjoy. He could have spent a lifetime kissing her. Her lips were warm and pliant, full and giving.

"Are you sure it's not too soon?" He gulped in air, wondered if he could be gentle, wondered if he could be all she needed.

"I'm fine."

"Oh, baby, you are definitely fine." He scooped her up in his arms, noted the surprised look on her face. "Nervous?"

"A little. There's something about the way you look. Desire and danger and power. It's exciting in a sort of forbidden way, you know? It makes a woman—"

"A woman?" he interrupted.

"Me. It makes me curious…and nervous…and excited."

He felt his mouth stretch into a grin, felt his ego swell. Hell, his whole damned body was swelling. He held her higher on his chest. His heart thundered like hoofbeats when she tightened her arm around his neck. "I like a curious woman."

And he loved watching bravado war with shyness. He wouldn't have thought his Emily would be shy.

He let her slide down his body until her feet touched the floor. For all his teasing, he was nervous, too.

This was Emily. The girl he'd thought of off and on for a lot of years. The one who'd etched a single, powerful memory in his mind with a simple act of kindness. The woman who'd carried his brother's babies. The woman he'd never dreamed would be sharing his bed.

He rested his hands on her shoulders, smoothed them over the soft sleeves of her sweater, linked his fingers with hers. And standing in the soft lamplight of his bedroom, he looked his fill.

Emily tilted her head back, aching for him. Why was he just standing there, looking at her? "Cheyenne?"

He let go of her hands, wrapped them around her hips and tilted her forward, against his arousal. She sucked in a breath, bit down on her bottom lip.

"Let me do that for you." He pressed his lips to hers, nipped lightly, teased and seduced. It was a kiss filled with passion and restraint. A kiss that felt both brand-new and familiar at once.

His hands slid up her sides, pushing her sweater up. He had her bra unhooked and his hands on her skin before she'd even registered the process.

A kernel of unease brought her out of the moment when she felt the damp nursing pads slide against her skin and fall to the floor.

She groaned and he kissed her forehead, her cheeks, pulled her sweater up and off, pressed his lips to the upper swell of her breasts. "You're beautiful. Every single part of you is so damned beautiful."

His words were spaced apart as though each syllable was exquisite torture, and her nerves settled some.

There was no place for embarrassment between them.

She wanted this man more than she wanted air to breathe.

He made her feel cherished with his reverent touch, his words, his single-minded attention. His velvety brown eyes roamed her like a caress, filled with approval and appreciation.

"Lie back," he said, and eased her onto the bed, undressing her and then himself. He kept his boxer shorts on and she started to comment on the unfairness of that, but he moved her against his side, his chest brushing her breasts, his fingers dancing gently over her sensitized skin, and she lost every thought in her head.

"I guess a woman fresh from the beauty shop ought to be appreciated."

"I guess."

She'd indulged in a day of pampering. And it wasn't

over. He seemed determined to extend that pampering into the night. The feel of his fingers combing through her hair raised chills on her skin. The pad of his thumb stroking her jaw made her burn.

Slowly, oh, so slowly, he caressed her neck, her shoulders, brushed the outer swell of her breast, taking his time, his gaze feasting.

"Shouldn't you turn out the light?" Her breast size had evened out some, but they still weren't perfect.

He shook his head. He was propped on an elbow beside her, gazing down at her as though she were a goddess.

"I want to see you."

"I'm not…my body's not…" *Firm* she would have said, but he laid a finger over her lips, then replaced it with his own lips, sipping, stroking, worshiping. His tongue swept the seam of her lips, yet never entered.

"Your body's perfect." He said the words against her mouth, then cupped her hip, drew her closer to his arousal, slipped his hand over the swell of her behind. "Soft and warm. Just right."

Oh, he made her feel just right. She knew she wasn't model material, but she wanted to be beautiful for him tonight.

Emotions welled up so strong she felt a lump rise in her throat, felt her eyes burn. She didn't know why. There was no reason for tears.

She reached for him, wrapped her arms around him, held him as tightly as she could, wondering if he could feel the emotions all but bursting inside her.

"Easy," he murmured. "We've got all night."

Oh, but they didn't. The babies would wake soon. And if he didn't hurry up and finish what he'd started—actually what *she'd* started—she would surely die.

"I think I'd like you to hurry a little."

His lips canted into a sexy smile that made her stomach flutter. "A little?" The maddening man stroked her from neck to knees, slowly, thoroughly, setting her ablaze.

"A lot." Was that her voice? All breathy and panting?

His lips followed the path of his hands. "Uh-uh. Relax, Ms. Business Lady. I've a mind to be the chairman tonight."

He could be the president of the United States for all she cared. She just wanted him to hurry.

And in the next instant she decided hurrying wasn't quite so important. His clever lips were doing something incredible to her palm, her wrist, the underside of her arm. And always, always, those deep-brown eyes watched her. Maybe they could go ahead and linger just a bit. Savoring was a good thing. And that was exactly what he was doing to her. Savoring. Thoroughly. Reverently. With a skill that astonished as much as it thrilled.

She closed her eyes, reveling in the sensations, and when his lips brushed the inside of her thigh, she nearly shot off the bed. Her hips arched and her hands fisted in his hair.

"I don't think—"

"That's right. Don't think." He kissed her in the

most intimate way a man could kiss a woman. Softly, surely. And Emily felt the blood roar in her head, pound in every secret pulse point in her body. No man had ever done this to her. She'd never let anyone so close, so intimately close.

It wasn't a matter of letting Cheyenne. He simply took.

And he gave.

Oh, he gave. Without apology, without hesitation, without expectations, with skill and verve and gentleness. She couldn't stand it, felt as though she were flying, soaring among the stars.

She tugged at his shoulders, needing...needing... "I need..."

He eased up her body. "Shh. I know what you need, baby."

She wrapped her arms around his shoulders, her legs around his waist. Her hands stroked everywhere she could reach, her lips pressing kisses to his jaw, his hair, his cheek and at last his mouth. With more haste than finesse, she managed to rid him of his boxer shorts.

"Now. Please, I need you now."

Her eyes were squeezed shut. She tried to find an anchor in the storm that raged inside her. She'd never felt so out of control. It scared her.

She moaned, pressed against him, tried to tell him with her body what her tongue couldn't seem to form into words.

"Look here, trouble."

His voice, deep and soft and raw with passion,

reached out and wrapped around her. She opened her eyes.

And saw her own desire reflected back.

Slowly, oh, so slowly, he entered her. She couldn't look away from him. She was falling, falling into his eyes, this man, his touch, his soul. She felt every slow slide of his body joining with hers.

She tried to hold back, to savor, but the sensations were too much. Her body pulsed, throbbed, and desire grabbed her in the throes of something incredibly radiant, incredibly blinding as the orgasm ripped through her, turned her blood to fire and her limbs to liquid.

He held himself still, pressed higher, harder, letting her ride the wave, waiting, just waiting. The ripples seemed to go on and on.

Coherency had barely returned before he was sweeping her up again, moving, stroking.

She hadn't known her body could respond like this and so soon. But that electrifying sensation was building again. He kissed her, drank from her lips, stroked her with an intoxicating expertise she was helpless to resist.

Oh, this man knew exactly what to do, when to do it.

"Cheyenne..." She didn't know what she was asking for. An anchor to cling to? A map of what was to come? The feelings roiling inside her frightened her. She didn't understand. Didn't have experience. Was flying blind.

"I'm right here. Hold on to me now." He slipped his hand between them, stroked the very core of her femininity and thrust high and hard, faster and faster. Her body spasmed again and again. Colors exploded behind her lids. A kaleidoscope of desire and love.

And when she thought she could feel no more, he took her higher still, pushed, demanded, hovered with her at the very brink of madness, then toppled them both into the abyss.

WHEN HIS BRAIN cleared enough for him to remember his own name, Cheyenne swore. He rolled with her, tucked her against his side, stroked her damp brow. "Are you okay?"

"Mmm-hmm."

"I should be horsewhipped. I should have been more careful with you."

She reached up and covered his lips with her fingers. His heart thudded all over again. Just a simple touch and he lost control.

"I'm fine. More than fine."

"Are you sure?"

She pushed him to his back, rolled with him, propped her crossed arms on his chest, her soft hair falling forward to tickle his shoulders. Aligning herself on top of him, she gave a wiggle that had his body jumping to life.

Hell on fire, that had never happened before.

Her green eyes were full of spunk and sparkle. "Do I need to prove how okay I am?"

He ran his hands over the curve of her spine, cupped her bottom, pressed her against his reawakening arousal.

"Mmm," she murmured.

His heart swelled in a way that scared him to death. He brought her face to his, kissed her with every ounce of tenderness he could muster.

When he eased back, her eyes were wet with tears.

"Damn it, I did hurt you."

"No," she whispered. "I just feel...happy." She gave a watery laugh, rolled off him and snuggled against his side. "You could bottle those kisses. Potent stuff."

He still wasn't convinced. He'd never had a woman go all misty when he'd kissed her. "Just the kisses?"

"Well, the rest of it, too. I don't mind telling you that was pretty incredible. I've never..."

"Never what?"

His arm tightened around her, holding her close. Her hand idly stroked his chest, back and forth.

"Um, nobody's ever kissed me in...in that other way."

His being the first to give her a new experience made him feel special. Possessive.

"Thanks," she whispered.

God, she made him feel ten feet tall. "It was my pleasure, trouble."

She gave his chest a light pinch. "Don't you make fun of me."

"Never." He kissed her hair to show her he was dead serious. "I like being your first."

"When I was a girl, I used to dream that you *would* be my first."

His hand stopped in midstroke on her arm, resumed.

"I'm glad I didn't know that. I'd have gone to jail for sure."

She smiled against his side, her eyelashes tickling his chest. "You were a tough guy. I don't think I could have talked you into initiating me sexually."

He was damned glad she hadn't put him to the test. He'd like to think he would have resisted, not stolen her innocence. But Emily had always had a potent effect on him.

"You never speak about your mom," she murmured.

Hell, from one explosive subject to another. Then again, being with Emily was like sitting on a powder keg. One wrong move, and she could ignite emotions he'd spent a lifetime keeping a lid on.

"You don't have to tell me about her if you don't want to."

"Do you remember seeing her?"

"Once. She was very beautiful."

"Yes. And social. I think that's what my father fell for. She looked like a delicate flower with a waterfall of raven hair. I remember her dancing. It was like she didn't walk anywhere, she floated or danced."

"And your dad fell in love with her spirit?"

"Probably. And ended up killing it. Their marriage wasn't accepted by my mother's people. My dad was a dreamer. I think my mom counted on him taking her away, figured they'd have these grand adventures together, traveling and living on fun. But fun didn't pay the bills. We hardly had anything."

He pulled the sheet over them when he felt her

shiver. "She started drinking, and their relationship went downhill from there. She didn't dance anymore, or laugh. She just drank, let herself fall apart, sank into a depression that sucked the beauty out of her face and heart. And he left her."

"And took Jimmy with him?"

"Yes. She drove her car off a bridge a couple years after the divorce. They said it was an accident. There weren't any skid marks, though."

Emily tightened her arms around him.

"Her sister, Uncle John's first wife, was with her."

"Oh, no."

"It was a while before I could face him. I felt responsible, like I should have been a better son or something, that somehow I could have pulled her out of her depression, out of the downward spiral I could see happening."

"It wasn't your fault!"

He nearly smiled. Her voice was so adamant. His Emily. Siding with the underdog.

"Uncle John said the same thing. He came to me, said it was our people's way to forgive and forget, that Ma'heo'o forgives all." His gut twisted as his mind fast-forwarded to another relationship. "That's what I tried to convey to Jimmy the last time I called him. I couldn't make him listen and it tore me up. My uncle said to be patient and wait it out. I waited too long."

"Jimmy had some responsibility in that, Cheyenne."

"Yeah. But it doesn't make it hurt any less."

She pressed her lips to his side, slid over on top of

him, tenderly settled her mouth against his. It was a kiss of forgiveness, as though she could give him Jimmy's apology through the sip of her lips, the breath of her soul.

Just like she'd brought the babies to him, giving him the lives of the children of his brother.

He wondered if she knew how much she had indeed healed him.

"If I could take the hurt away, I would," she whispered against his lips.

She was amazing. She humbled him, made him feel so much.

"You have, baby. More than you know." And because he didn't have the words, he rolled with her, used his body as tenderly as he could to convey how special she was, the sunshine she'd brought into his life, the miracles. Softly, silently, he let his body speak, and gave her his soul.

CHEYENNE WASN'T IN BED when Emily awoke. They'd been up twice last night to feed the twins and made love again each time. She hated to admit it, but she was wrecked. She'd been a zombie before with just the middle-of-the-night feedings. Add great sex, and she was nearly in a class with the walking dead.

But oh, it was worth it. Her body hummed. The spray of the shower felt sensual against her skin, the fresh highlights in her hair looked brighter.

She checked on the babies, sent up a silent prayer of thanks that they were asleep once again and made her way to the kitchen for coffee. She really shouldn't wish their little lives away in slumber, but they were truly a handful when they were awake.

Still, she wouldn't trade a moment of their precious lives. Three months ago she'd never have imagined how drastically her world would turn, how full her heart would be.

She stepped out onto the porch and saw Cheyenne sitting on the wicker bench, steam rising from the mug in his hand.

She lowered herself beside him as though they met this way every morning of their lives. Just like a truly married couple.

"Hi," she said softly.

"Hi, yourself." He glanced at her as though not quite sure how to act and waiting to take his cue from her.

She didn't want him to be sorry. And she didn't want to go backward. She wanted to go forward. They had until the end of January before her maternity leave was up.

Why not enjoy what they had together? Why deny themselves that incredible pleasure?

She put her hand on his thigh and heard him let out a breath. He covered her hand and they sat in silence, enjoying the brisk morning air.

The horses were out in the coral, gathered in a little knot like ladies at a morning coffee klatch exchanging juicy gossip.

"Are you going in to work today?"

"No. My uncle is bringing some of the children from the reservation later today to ride horses."

"Oh. I guess I didn't realize your stock was the gentle type that children would ride."

"Stony trains them. When he's finished with them, they'll stand docile as a lamb or run like the wind, depending on which signal you give."

"That's nice. I imagine it's a treat for the kids. Do they come often?"

"Usually once a month. I postponed last month's visit because of the babies."

"Oh, I'm sorry. You shouldn't have done that."

"It's better this way. That's why I put the lights up. Figured it'd be more festive. I meant to warn you yesterday, but something sidetracked me."

She gave him an intimate smile. "I enjoyed that sidetrack. And I'm a pretty spontaneous sort. What can I do to help?"

"Nothing. Uncle John's got it covered. He'll bring meat and barbecue some burgers and hot dogs. He's the biggest kid in the bunch. He looks so serious half the time, but he's really a softy."

"I like him."

"And he likes you."

"I could tell that family's important to him."

Cheyenne nodded. "He has deep roots in the people of our tribe, though he straddles both worlds. He's a deeply traditional, yet forward-thinking man, does big business with the oil and gas companies and has a portfolio that would make your eyes pop."

"You're kidding. Will he give me stock tips?"

He smiled. "I imagine he would if you asked. He gives them to me."

She sighed. "Your uncle startled me the other day when he showed up in the doorway. He didn't say a lot, but I could tell he was pleased with the babies."

"He has a soft heart for children. He doesn't have children of his own, but with the Cheyenne, there are no orphans."

"That's beautiful. You're lucky to have him."

"Took me a while to realize that."

"You're referring to your cocky youth again?"

"I suppose. Can't go back and change the past, though." He took a sip of coffee, watched the horses nuzzling each other. "Looks like the weather'll hold out, so I've retrofitted the wagon and we'll take the children on a sleigh ride, then come back and roast some marshmallows."

Her eyes were wide and her insides felt giddy. "A sleigh ride?"

He grinned down at her. "Yeah. Wanna go?"

"Will there be room?"

"It's a big wagon. I'll load it with bales of hay I've got warming in the barn. If you wrap the twins up real good and sit between a couple of the bales, they should be warm enough."

"I'd love to go. We'll sing Christmas carols. Oh, I just adore this season."

This would be her first Christmas without her sister. They usually had a simple day—a gift exchange, Debbie busy in the kitchen, Emily's contribution snitching bites of this and that or getting in the way.

But here in Shotgun Ridge, there was so much going on. The love and community spirit was palpable.

And now a sleigh ride. She hopped up, nearly spilling Cheyenne's coffee.

"Hey, where are you going?"

"I've got to get me and the kids ready for company."

FROM THE WARMTH of the kitchen, Emily watched Cheyenne with the children his uncle had brought out in a minivan. When they were mounted on horses, he led them around the corral, stopping to answer questions, tie a shoe, dry a tear when one of the boys got too exuberant and fell in the dirt. He was such a kind man. So good with children.

The Christmas lights strung on the barn were lit. Icicles hung from the eaves, dripping color. John White Cloud was flipping burgers on a grill atop an old barrel filled with charcoal.

The yard rang with laughter and love and a peace that made her sigh. So different from her life in the city, with its bustle, shrill phones and nonstop pace.

So much had changed in her life in so short a time.

She looked down at her own babies, cradled close to her chest in the papoose John and his wife, Jenny White Cloud, had given her. In her wildest dreams, she never knew she could love something so much as these babies. They were her heart.

But they were Cheyenne's heart, too. She could see that clearly—in the middle of the night when he sat half-asleep feeding them, in the morning when he smiled and cooed and played with them before he left for work, in all the little glances and touches, it radiated from him.

They'd taken their relationship to a new level, but that didn't solve their problems. It only complicated issues. Or did it?

He was a man with a man's urges. She was here, a woman and available.

He gave her compliments and pretty words, but he never indicated his heart was involved, never mentioned her staying past her maternity leave.

And when that time came, what then? She would be taking the babies with her. Unless he surprised her, insisted she honor the marriage. What if he blocked her from taking the kids out of the state?

In her heart of hearts, she knew he would never do such a thing.

The problem was, she would still be breaking his heart by separating him from the kids. And that was the last thing she wanted to do.

She'd never intended to hurt anybody, but she was terribly afraid someone was going to get hurt, anyway.

If he asked her to stay, would she?

She closed her eyes, pictured her corner office with its bank of windows, pictured her art deco condo, tickets to the theater, Jonathan's Hair Salon where she had a standing appointment every four weeks for her hair and every two weeks for her nails.

It made her head hurt.

When the time came, would he ask her to stay for the children? Could she give up a life she loved if the man in question hadn't asked for her heart?

Hadn't given her his?

Chapter Thirteen

"We need a Christmas tree," Emily said as they drove to church the next morning. Now that they'd started taking the babies out, Pastor Dan had told them there was no excuse for sleeping in on the Lord's day.

As if anyone could sleep with twin infants in the house. Cheyenne wondered if he'd ever get over feeling tired.

He glanced at Emily who was still glowing like an excited kid over the sleigh ride he'd taken her and the kids on last night. She was in the Christmas spirit now.

"I usually don't get one."

"Why not?"

He shrugged, wishing her wool skirt hadn't ridden up so high on her thigh. The sight was playing havoc with his concentration. "It's just me. Seemed a waste."

"It's not just you this year."

True, he thought, but if he bought a tree, built memories, how would he feel next year when he was alone again? "I'll bring one home later. Unless you want to go with me and pick it out." Another memory. Maybe she'd say no.

"We could go after church."

"We could." *Damn it.*

"Do you have ornaments or will we need to buy those, too?"

He sighed, responding to the excitement in her voice. She really did come alive with all the hoopla of the season. He wanted to give her everything her heart desired.

"I have some in the shed." Leftover frills from the one year his house *had* been decorated, decked out with the best ornaments money could buy.

The year Linda had been there.

Too bad it had been wasted. She'd left two days before he'd given her the diamond ring that rested in the jeweler's box beneath the tree, leaving the lavishly festive house looking gaudy and cluttered and sad.

He hadn't put up a tree since. The most he did was string lights on the house and the barn for the kids who came out to ride.

"We'll take a picture of the twins under the tree."

She was so excited, as though the season itself flowed in her veins. He felt like a killjoy with his depressing thoughts.

He glanced over at her and smiled. "No bare-bottom shots. Hunter'll never forgive you."

She laughed. "Okay, okay. Suppose he'll object to that little elf suit I picked up at Carly McCall's shop?"

"Elf suit? Looked like a red snowsuit to me." The town was really growing, Cheyenne thought as they traveled down Main Street. Carly McCall's boutique was one of the newest additions. She'd come to town a while back with her little girl, Jewel, and fallen in love with the contractor hired to build houses and the new hotel. They'd already built a fancy home out on a piece of property Jake McCall had bought from the Malones.

Cheyenne suspected Ozzie Peyton and his cohorts had had a hand in the romance. Those old men were a menace. Hell, hadn't they done the same thing with him and Emily? Given her the wrong address and maneuvered them to be right under the same roof?

He didn't know whether to curse them or thank them.

He had an idea a couple of months from now he'd be cursing.

He pulled into the church parking lot, which was already filled with pickups, and got out to unbuckle the twins.

"Want the seats?"

"No. Let's just hold them."

He nodded and passed Hunter to her, then gathered Alicia, making sure the blanket covered her face from the chill wind and bright sun.

If somebody had told him months ago that he'd be attending church services as a family man, he'd have locked them up and called a psychiatrist to make an evaluation.

Friends and neighbors swarmed around them, swallowing Emily in the crowd, separating them. Ladies sighed over the babies and wanted to relieve him of his burden.

His reluctance to relinquish the baby was keen. She felt so warm and right cuddled in his arms. Iris Brewer's will was stronger than his own, because she whisked the baby right off. The woman had grandchildren of her own, he grumbled to himself—Hannah's little ones—yet she seemed to want to adopt his, as well.

He couldn't get too worked up. This was his town. These were his people. He loved them all as though they were blood. And they cared about him and his own.

They made it through the church service—Dan Lucas was in fine form, telling jokes from the pulpit. Cheyenne would say one thing about the preacher, he definitely kept his parishioners entertained. Nobody even thought to nod off. But there was a spiritual element, too, something that touched the soul.

The potluck after the services was a weekly standard that felt familiar and comfortable. He looked around for Emily, saw her in the middle of a clutch of women, arranging pies and cakes, ham and fried chicken and salads.

A single man in town would never go hungry. All he had to do was come to church and he could eat enough to last him the week.

Wyatt Malone stood next to him. "Looks like your wife's found a project she can sink her teeth into."

His wife. The two words gave him a punch in the heart.

Cheyenne raised a brow, watching as Opal and Mildred pouted because Ozzie and Lloyd were holding the twins. "What project is that?"

"The Christmas play Dan's organizing. Emily decided it needed an advertising touch and claimed she was just the woman to get the project off the ground."

He felt a smile pulling his lips. She was all but in a huddle with the other women, the preacher at the center of the discussion. "Don't recall us needing to advertise it in years past."

"I mentioned that," Ethan Callahan said as he and Stony joined the circle of men. "Eden told me to hush up—" he shot a glance at Stony as though the man should speak to his wife about her bossiness "—and Dora said since she knows church business, seeing as she's a preacher's daughter, and Emily's the top of her field in advertising and should certainly know a thing or two, that I should go off and find guy stuff to do."

"You'll notice my wife wasn't mentioned in the dressing-down," Wyatt commented smugly.

"Pretty cocky for being so henpecked," Ethan challenged.

"I'm not henpecked."

"Yeah? It was your wife who seconded the girls' suggestion, told me to come on over here because you know your place."

Wyatt grinned. "Hell of a woman."

Love, Cheyenne thought. It was all around him. In the eyes of his best friends as they exaggerated their wives' transgressions.

Jake McCall, the town's building contractor, came

over to join them, rubbing his forehead as though a headache brewed. "I've been banished to the rooster section."

"*Now* who's calling us roosters?" Stony wanted to know.

"That would be *my* wife." Carly. "They're talking about building a stage set. Before long they'll be drawing up plans for a full-scale theater. Man alive, I've got more work than my crew can keep up with as it is."

Cheyenne glanced over at the women, his own Emily right in the middle of them all. She'd always known how to stir things up in this town. Instead of meeting with censure, though, as she'd feared, it was obvious that she was met with love and respect and admiration.

Oh, God, when she left, there would be a hole in his life. Much bigger, deeper, wider, than the one she'd left when they were kids.

He should be stepping back from her. Damned if he didn't want to move closer.

EMILY DROVE HOME from town, pleased with the plans she'd set in motion last Sunday after church. The play was coming along nicely, every child in the Sunday-school class cast in a part, no matter how small. Her own twins were on standby to play the part of baby Jesus in the manger. They figured they could decide at the last minute between Hunter, Alicia, Sarah Stratton and Ryan Callahan. As they were all under five months, they wouldn't be aware enough to have their feelings hurt if they failed to snag the starring role. The toss of the dice would depend on which one had the most pleasant disposition on opening night.

But for the rest of the little ones, who were so excited and practicing their lines diligently, Emily wanted them to have their five minutes of fame. And the more people who came, the more donations the church would get.

So she'd sent notices around the county, contacted the local papers and the radio station. After all, the stations went all out advertising rodeos; might as well give their production the same hype.

She'd also designed a new sign for the church, built by Jake McCall, and ordered magnetic, weather-resistant letters so events and times could be posted for everyone driving through town to see.

And since she'd been so caught up in the advertising, she'd found herself organizing the rehearsals, as well. After all, she did know a thing or two about production.

Next up, she'd need to turn her thoughts to the drive-through Nativity production. They'd have live animals, a camel perhaps. Her mind was buzzing.

With her trunk filled with gifts she'd picked up in town, she felt her spirits soar. She'd never looked forward to a holiday as much as she did this one.

Emergency lights flashing on the highway up ahead made her heart skip a beat, then race in dread. An accident, she realized as she got closer. Slick roads and a curve taken too fast.

An image of an accident she hadn't witnessed but

could see clearly flashed in her mind—Jimmy's sport utility van wedged beneath a semi, life seeping out of her sister's veins.

Had they held each other in those last minutes? Had they gone quickly? Emily hadn't been able to ask.

She glanced in the rearview mirror at the twins sleeping peacefully in their car seats, feeling love swell. Tragedy had gifted her with those two little lives to care for.

She slowed and brought her attention back to the road. Her heart rammed against her ribs and her hands shook. She felt sick.

The emergency light on top of Cheyenne's Bronco flashed like a strobe in the late-afternoon light. She eased her foot off the gas pedal, then drove on past. He had his hands full; he didn't need onlookers.

But oh, she ached for him.

Her husband. The rescuer.

WHEN HE CAME HOME, Cheyenne didn't say a word. He stood over the crib where the twins slept, oblivious to the near tragedy he'd witnessed.

Teenagers, he thought. They'd sustained a fair number of injuries, but the doctors said they would recover. The worst part had been notifying the parents. God, he hated that part of his job.

The kids had been lucky. The car had flipped, but a snowbank had cushioned some of the impact. Seat belts had done their job. Otherwise, two sets of parents would have had a Christmas filled with mourning, instead of joy.

He fought not to let the sadness swamp him. His own brother was lost to him, wouldn't be spending the holiday exclaiming over gifts, sharing kisses and food and the incredible joy of filling his arms with babies. It didn't matter that it had been years since he'd spent a holiday with his brother.

There had always been hope.

He'd known Jimmy was out there somewhere.

Now that hope was gone. He had his brothers' children, instead.

He touched each of their little cheeks, careful not to wake them. The feel of them, the smell of them, filled him with emotions he couldn't name.

A gift. Yes, Emily had given him a gift. Because he could feel Jimmy, see him, in these babies.

He turned, saw Emily standing silently in the doorway, hall light spilling over her blond hair.

Her eyes were soft and filled with compassion. He'd seen her drive by, had felt such relief that his own family was safe, then felt guilty for the thought when two young people were bleeding and crying in pain.

So much pain in the world.

"Are you hungry?" she asked softly.

He shook his head, went to her, reached for her, held her with arms that wanted to shake and strained to be gentle.

She soothed him with her hands on his back, rubbed.

"I need you," he whispered.

"I'm right here."

He gazed down at her. *But for how long,* was what

they were both thinking. Life could snatch loved ones away in an instant. Job responsibilities could wrench a family apart. God, his head hurt to think.

So he kissed her, lost himself in her soft lips and giving spirit. He drank from her, easing the horror of the wreckage that still plagued his mind.

How many times had he come home to an empty house, the screams of mourning ringing in his ears and no one to distract his mind.

"Will dinner keep?" he asked quietly.

"For as long as you want."

"Then help me shut out the night."

TWO DAYS LATER, Emily was still thinking about the night of the accident. He'd needed her, and for once she'd known it without a doubt, felt it deep in her bones, in the touch of his hands and the whisper of his lips. Their lovemaking had been different; he'd seemed different. It was as though love sang in every sigh and touch.

Something had shifted between them. She was certain of it, yet he'd pulled back from her. He was different, quieter, helping more and asking less.

She wanted to shake him. Instead, she scoured the sink and watched the clock. She'd faxed the last of the changes for the cosmetics ad. It was good. Dynamite. Better than anything the competitors had come up with. Never mind that she was biased.

When the phone rang, she jumped and the sponge went flying. Snatching up a towel, she gave her hands a swipe to dry them and dived for the receiver.

"Hey, kiddo, you did it," Dave Kimble said.

"We got the account?" Excitement bubbled inside her, roared in her ears, made her stomach lurch. She held her breath, trying to act professional, wanted to shriek and dance and laugh like a loon.

"Yep. All sewed up in time for Christmas. I'm authorized to tell you there's a cushy promotion with your name on it as soon as you get back from maternity leave."

She did shriek then and listened to her associate laugh. She barely heard the rest of the details he imparted, and when she hung up the phone, she wasn't altogether sure if she'd even told Dave goodbye.

Her insides were a tangle of butterflies. She wanted to leap with joy, shout it from the rooftops. She did a little dance around the kitchen.

Yes! Vice president! Ten long years of hard work and fifteen-hour days had paid off.

Cheyenne walked into the kitchen and caught her dancing like a fairy. She leaped into his arms, wrapping her legs around his waist.

"Whoa, trouble. What's all the excitement?"

"I got the account. I've courted them for two years and I did it!"

"Congratulations."

She gave him a smacking kiss on his lips, then slid down his body, her face stretched in such a wide grin it almost hurt. "I'll have you know you're looking at the new vice president of Cockran Advertising."

"So you'll be leaving, then." His tone was casual.

He stepped back, picked up the soapy sponge that was still sitting on the floor where it had landed.

The question stopped her, brought her back to earth. She hadn't thought past the excitement of the moment, of hearing Dave tell her she'd gotten the job. Hadn't thought about how it would affect her life—life as it was now.

She landed from her high with a thud as the reality of here and now settled around her. She looked at Cheyenne, trying to see past his question, but his handsome face masked his emotions. He could just as easily be asking her if she was going to town, instead of all the way to Seattle.

"What do you think?" She wished he'd tell her what he felt. He'd never pressured her, never asked for more.

"It's a great opportunity for you, Emily. I know you've worked hard for this account, this promotion." He touched her cheek, then took his hat off the peg by the door. "We should do something to celebrate your success."

"Cheyenne—"

A baby started to cry. She sighed.

"Want me to check?" he asked.

She shook her head. "No. You go ahead and see to your horses."

It was clear he was anxious to get out of the house. Her confidence wavered. She was so sure he felt something deeper. He had helped her with the babies, which was all she'd asked of him. Was he simply honoring his bargain to her?

Chapter Fourteen

Cheyenne went out to the barn, feeling his heart twist. The scent of hay and molasses oats, leather and horses wrapped him in a cloak of familiarity, yet the usual comfort it evoked seemed to be missing.

This was his dream—this ranch, this town, his job. He'd been happy here. If he'd been lonely, he didn't like to admit it.

Funny, he hadn't felt that loneliness since Emily had come. His world had come alive.

She'd made him come alive.

How could he go back to his solitary existence when she left?

He reached for the latch on the wooden stall door. The sound of Emily yelling his name, her voice filled with a mother's terror, had him racing back into the house.

He took the porch steps in one leap, nearly tore the door off its hinges, his heart thundering in dread.

She was still in the kitchen, but she had Alicia in her arms.

In a single glance he searched the room, Emily, the baby, looking for blood or danger.

''What is it?''

''She's burning up. She's so still, lifeless. Oh, my God, Cheyenne, something bad's wrong with her.''

He touched his fingers to the baby's downy cheek. It felt hot, but he couldn't tell how hot because his fingers were cold. The flushed skin and listlessness, the shallow breathing, though, told its own story.

''Get your coat. I'll get Hunter.''

He didn't even take the time to phone the clinic. In minutes he had them bundled out to the truck and strapped in. Hunter was screaming his lungs out at being snatched from sleep and thrust rudely into the cold.

Emily was terrified. He could see it in her face, hear it in the trembling of her voice as she spoke to the baby in her arms.

She didn't ask him any questions, just let him take the lead.

And he did.

He slammed the truck in gear and spun out of the yard, the knobby tires barely slipping in the snow. Snatching up the mike to the two-way radio as he navigated the driveway, he switched to the public frequency.

''Chance, this is Cheyenne, come back.''

Most of the neighbors monitored the radio, including the doctor. Half the men in town were volunteer firefighters, and when someone had a need, everyone pitched in. Cheyenne knew the radio would be on at Chance's house, as well as at the clinic.

"Hey, Cheyenne," Chance responded. "What's up?"

"I'm coming in hot to the clinic. One of the twins has a fever."

"How high?"

"I didn't stop to take it. It's high."

"She conscious?"

Damn it!

He glanced at Emily, saw the tears in her eyes, the fear. He felt that fear himself.

"Yes." He tried to keep his voice impersonal, steady. Hell, he was a professional, dealt with crises every day. They weren't personal, though. And this was. "She's awake, but listless." His voice shook. Hunter was screaming in the back seat.

Alicia was utterly still and quiet in Emily's arms.

Oh, God, that wasn't a good sign.

"I'll be standing by," Chance said.

He pressed the accelerator.

By the time they reached town, Chance was at the clinic. The doctor quickly took the baby out of Emily's arms. Hunter was still crying. "Is he sick, too?"

"No," Emily said, her voice scratchy with emotion. "Just Alicia. What's wrong with her?"

"Give me a minute with her."

She followed. Chance shook his head. "Cheyenne, take her out to the waiting room."

"No. I have to stay with her." Her insides were twisted into knots. She'd never been so scared in her life. She'd been dancing a jig in the kitchen, and her baby daughter had been burning up with fever.

Cheyenne put his arm around her. "Come on, Em. We need to get Hunter settled down and give Chance some room. If Alicia starts responding to Hunter's distress, it'll make Chance's job harder."

She knew he was right. Oh, this was one of those instances where she simply didn't have enough arms to go around. She lifted Hunter out of his seat, cradled him, shushed him, paced with him.

Soon afterward, friends and neighbors streamed through the doors of the clinic. They'd heard the fear in Cheyenne's voice. They felt they had a stake in the children's lives. Someone might need a shoulder, a cup of coffee, a baby-sitter.

Emily looked around at the love in the small waiting room.

Looked around at all she'd be giving up.

Cheyenne came up behind her, circled his arms around both her and Hunter, rested his cheek on top of her head. She leaned into him, grateful for his strength.

It seemed forever until Chance finally came back into the waiting room, Alicia bundled in his arms. "There's a little girl here who's looking to say hi to her folks."

Emily thrust Hunter into Cheyenne's arms, rushed over to gather her baby girl in her arms—the baby girl who was staring sleepily up at her, happily sucking on a pacifier.

"The fever?" She touched her fingers to Alicia's soft cheek.

"It's down. She'll be fine."

As Chance explained his theory on what had caused the fever to spike, cautioned her to watch for a rash in a few days' time, she tuned out. Her baby was fine. Overwhelmed, overwrought, she sat right down on the floor and cried.

A DOUBLE WHAMMY. Twice in the space of an hour yesterday, he'd feared losing both Emily and Alicia, one to her job, the other to a fever. His heart hadn't recovered.

He'd slept in snatches beside the crib. By dawn he was fairly certain the baby's crisis was indeed past.

Now his mood was nasty.

So he was working it off in the barn, his uncle giving him plenty of space, not speaking.

That almost made him angrier.

He'd cleaned and oiled every piece of equipment in the tack room. Bridles hung in military precision, bits were arranged by size and shape, saddles draped horn to cantle-binding over a wooden sawhorse.

"Aren't you talking this morning?" he snapped at John, and instantly regretted his tone.

"When a man has much on his mind, it is wise to give him room to think."

"Emily got the promotion she's worked so hard for."

John White Cloud laid down the currycomb he'd

been using on Lightning, came out of the stall and closed the wooden door. "So she will leave?"

"Yes. I'm happy for her."

"Are you?"

"Don't start with me, Uncle."

John stuck a piece of straw in the corner of his mouth, leaned a shoulder against the wall. "You have taken on the burdens of an entire county. You serve and protect all people—right down to Emily and the twins. Yet you ask nothing in return for yourself."

"That wasn't part of our bargain."

"And what if she wishes it so?"

"Didn't you hear me, Uncle? She's got the job she's been working for all her life."

"Do you want her to stay?"

"That's not the point."

"It is, yes. Ask," he counseled.

Cheyenne's heart thudded. "What if the answer's no?"

"The answer will be no unless you ask. You must risk."

And that was the crux of the matter.

He hadn't risked anything. He didn't have anything on the line. He hadn't asked her to stay.

He'd known going in that the marriage wasn't for keeps. When he'd asked Linda to stay all those years ago, she'd shut him down, and he'd vowed never to put himself in that position again.

And marriage to Emily *hadn't* put him there. They both knew the rules. Were biding their time.

But by God, he wanted to change the rules.

He had to take the risk, do the one thing he'd promised himself he wouldn't do. He had to put his heart on the line.

"If there were second chances," John said, "what would you wish for?"

"Family." It came out easily, without hesitation. He hadn't known the yearning was there, that it went so deep. His friends, Wyatt, Ethan and Stony, were living proof that love was real. It might not always be easy or tidy, but true love was beauty. It shone like the brightest star, clearly visible for anyone who cared to look.

When it was the right kind of love, like that of Ozzie Peyton and his late wife, Vanessa, it formed a foundation that would weather anything life could throw at it. Because love and families stood together, solid.

That was what Cheyenne wanted. And he wanted it with Emily and the twins.

But what if he was wrong about her feelings? He was a man who could tell if a perp was lying, was trained to notice subtle nuances.

And every nuance Emily projected was love. He couldn't be that wrong.

He turned to his uncle. "If I asked, would you take my ranch, see that the stock continues to build?"

John White Cloud studied his nephew. "If you do not ask, the answer is always no," he repeated.

Cheyenne wasn't one hundred percent sure, but he thought that meant yes. Maybe it was a "We'll see."

Right now, though, he had a powerful urge to seek out his wife.

He was dismayed to see that his yard had filled with vehicles while he was in the barn—Ozzie and his pals, the Bagley widows.

Damn it, he didn't have time for company!

He stopped inside the back door, cleared his throat. "Emily, can I have a word with you?"

Emily looked up. "Cheyenne. What's wrong?" She was on her feet, checking him as though looking for an injury. His heart clicked wide open.

Ah, to hell with the audience. It'd be all over town within an hour, anyway.

"I'm coming with you."

She frowned. "Coming with me where? I don't think we should take Alicia out so soon after her fever. That's why the play committee is meeting here and—"

"Not to the play, damn it. To Washington."

She stared at him. "Why?"

"Because you're my lady. My wife." He took a breath, tried to infuse some romance into his words. "I love you, damn it."

Somebody in the room groaned. He ignored them. Couldn't these people leave him to blunder in peace?

"You and those babies are my life, my heart. Losing you would be like losing a piece of myself. I lost my brother because of pride. I won't lose you and the babies."

"Cheyenne—"

"Nothing says I have to run for sheriff again. I can get a job in law enforcement in Seattle. And if you can't love me back, at least I'll be close to you and the kids."

Because he hadn't let her speak, she put a hand over his lips. "Ask me to stay."

"I don't expect that kind of sacrifice. This job offer is your dream. If I could give you the moon, I would. Just let me share your dream."

"Ask me," she repeated stubbornly.

Damn it. *If you don't ask, the answer is always no.* He glanced toward the door, saw his uncle there.

He still hadn't put anything on the line. He hadn't taken the chance of asking her to stay. He'd only offered to go.

He looked down at this woman who'd held his heart since she was a skinny little spitfire of fourteen. "Please stay with me."

"Yes."

His ears were ringing. He wasn't certain he'd heard. "Yes?"

"Oh, yes."

"What about the job?"

"I already turned it down. What do I need with a fussy title, anyway?"

"You quit? Emily, I can't let you—"

"Don't you start that bossy stuff, Bodine. Of course I didn't quit. I just moved my office is all. I have a perfectly good computer modem, telephone line and fax machine. No reason in the world why my home base can't be right here in Shotgun Ridge. Besides, I *did* get a promotion, and more money, to boot—with less work. I'm now Cockran Advertising's new consultant."

He blinked, trying to take it all in. "Will you be happy being a consultant?"

"Are you kidding? It's a dream job. I get the final say on all the projects, and everybody else has to do the work. Besides, I figured I'd need more free time with the kids and all the stuff that needs an advertising touch here in town. And then when the other babies come along—"

"Whoa, what other babies?"

"The ones we'll have, of course."

"Are you saying you're pregnant?"

"Not yet. But I was hoping to talk my handsome husband into working on the matter. I've been told I'm pretty persuasive."

He laughed, kissed her, whispered against her lips, "Do you realize you've just announced our personal business to a town full of matchmaking gossips?"

"Mmm. Do you think I shocked them?"

"Want me to ask?"

"No. I think you should kiss your wife."

He cupped her cheeks, pressed his lips to hers.

"I've dreamed of the day you would be my lady. You're everything to me, my heart and my soul."

"Oh, Cheyenne." Her eyes filled with tears and he gently brushed them away.

"*Nemehotâtse,* Emily." The softly spoken words in his native tongue had everyone in the room sighing, though only John White Cloud understood. Then Cheyenne translated, his voice tender and sincere, a declaration and a promise of a lifetime. "I love you."

OZZIE PEYTON wasn't aware he was holding hands with the Bagley widows until he found the need to reach for his handkerchief. Opal handed him hers.

He refused to be embarrassed over his show of emotion. A body could get misty if he was of a mind to, you bet. And when a plan came together this nicely, all wrapped up with a pretty bow shining with love, it was enough to make a man's chest just puff right out. You bet.

He glanced at his buddies, who'd abandoned their impromptu planning committee to watch love unfold.

"We done it again, boys," he said. "I'd say we got a purdy durn-good batting average. Ain't missed one yet."

The other geezers nodded, as did the Bagley widows. And every one of them figured with this winning record, they ought to strike while the branding iron was still hot.

And they had just the stubborn cuss in mind who needed a nudge.

*　*　*　*　*

Next month it's Chance's turn!
Don't miss Mindy Neff's
next installment in her
BACHELORS OF SHOTGUN RIDGE
miniseries.
#902
THE DOCTOR'S INSTANT FAMILY
Available December 2001
at a store near you.

Coming in December from

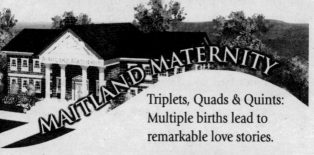

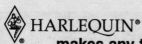

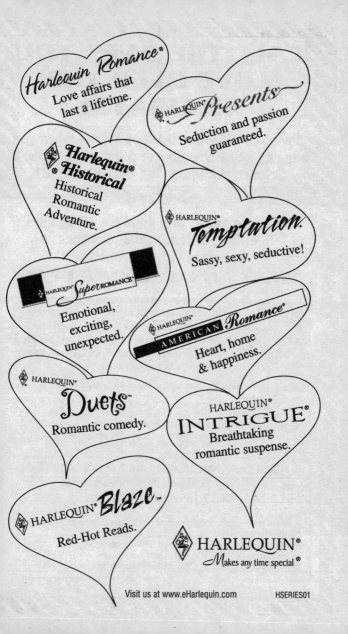

CALL THE ONES YOU LOVE OVER THE HOLIDAYS!

Save $25 off future book purchases when you buy any four Harlequin® or Silhouette® books in October, November and December 2001,

PLUS

receive a phone card good for 15 minutes of long-distance calls to anyone you want in North America!

WHAT AN INCREDIBLE DEAL!

Just fill out this form and attach 4 proofs of purchase (cash register receipts) from October, November and December 2001 books, and Harlequin Books will send you a coupon booklet worth a total savings of $25 off future purchases of Harlequin® and Silhouette® books, AND a 15-minute phone card to call the ones you love, anywhere in North America.

Please send this form, along with your cash register receipts as proofs of purchase, to:
In the USA: Harlequin Books, P.O. Box 9057, Buffalo, NY 14269-9057
In Canada: Harlequin Books, P.O. Box 622, Fort Erie, Ontario L2A 5X3
Cash register receipts must be dated no later than December 31, 2001.
Limit of 1 coupon booklet and phone card per household.
Please allow 4-6 weeks for delivery.

I accept your offer! Enclosed are 4 proofs of purchase.
Please send me my coupon booklet
and a 15-minute phone card:

Name: _____

Address: _____ City: _____

State/Prov.: _____ Zip/Postal Code: _____

Account Number (if available): _____

---

097 KJB DAGL
PHQ4013